African Beauty

African Beauty

Mark Weston

'He knew the taverns well in every town,
and every innkeeper and bar-maid,
better than he knew any leper or beggar.'

Geoffrey Chaucer, The Canterbury Tales

1

By the time I got back to the island she was gone.

Gone, that is, her physical form. Her imprint, the memory of her, remained etched in the islanders' minds.

And not only on this island. Men came from all the islands of the lake and from its distant shores to gaze from afar, to inhale the aura. Some paddled their own boats, abandoning their nets on the beaches and forgetting for a while the disappearing fish. Others crowded the ferries, the little motorised canoes that puttered between islets. They begged the ferrymen to make room for one more passenger, impoverished themselves to bribe those that stood firm. Every square inch was filled, luggage banned, benches thrown overboard to squeeze more bodies onto the puddled floor. The canoes' wooden flanks bulged under the pressure, creaked in noisy protest. One, in worse shape or more overloaded than the rest, sank within minutes of setting out. The passengers, non-swimming mainlanders who until they migrated to the fishing camps had seen water only down a well, would have drowned if the boat had gone down fifty yards farther out. They would have been eaten if a group of crocodiles basking on a nearby rock had been awoken by the commotion. As they waded back to shore they chattered excitedly, marvelling at their good fortune, their determination to board the next ferry made steelier still by the miracle.

Even now they talked of her, weeks after she had disappeared over the waves. Faces you strain to keep in your mind's eye are so slippery, so easy to forget, the very effort of preservation seeming to speed their pixellation. But not hers. Hers remained clearly visible in their heads. They talked of nothing else; it was as if they could *see* nothing else.

Only the pictures, which were all that was left for latecomers, were grainy. Whenever a phone had been aimed in her direction she had turned or hidden her face, like those tribespeople who believe a photograph steals a part of your soul. Would-be soul snatchers were forced to snap from the sidelines, and in what was an ill-lit barroom and with phones that were far from the latest model, the results were murky, the best of them no clearer than a reflection in the wind-riffled lake. In profile I could make out the glimmer of a cheekbone, the bescarved brow, the long neck held forward as she listened to the other girls. For the rest I had to ask those who had seen her, to tease out their memories, to encourage them, impossibly, to turn pictures into language. *Their* field of vision was filled with her vivid, searing image, like some blinding apparition of the Virgin; *I* had to rely on mere words.

They did their best. I had gone to the bar straight from the boat. Harry was there on his stool behind the yellow-painted counter, doling out bottles through the railings that shielded his stock from the swelling hordes of thieves. He had been away as well, he was saying; he'd just got back from that long-dead novelist's umpteenth memorial service. Harry loved a good story, and there was none better than the wrestler's. He was an emotional sort – he'd blub like a baby if your narrative had an unhappy ending, and had been known to cut a story short if it became too upsetting. The parable of the great wrestler is the saddest tale of all, and he felt he had to pay his respects to its author. During the service he had stood quietly at the back, his hands clasped below his ample belly. Once everybody had delivered their encomiums and left, he moved forward and left a book on the grave. He wouldn't tell me what the book was – that was between him and the novelist – only that it was 'a very old book, full of lovely stories.' He thought it would cheer the dead novelist up.

He asked about my own trip. I skimmed over the details. Harry was a demanding listener, and would have given me short shrift if I'd talked at length of my world-saving efforts. I told him instead about the shopkeeper I'd met in the capital who had offered me a night with his wife (an African custom I'd thought long-extinct) in return for helping him to pay off a debt he'd run up betting on European football. When I told Harry I'd rebuffed the offer - I couldn't risk any more compromising photos – his face elongated in disbelief.

'She wasn't interested, you mean,' he said with a chortle.

'She played no part in the negotiations,' I replied, diluting my Warthog with a drop of sugar cane gin. 'We didn't get as far as finding out what she thought of the proposal, although by all accounts she was an enthusiastic practitioner of her trade.'

Harry reached to switch on the television set perched on a stack of beer crates beside the bar. It was showing wrestling from America, the volume muted. 'Anyway, Hodge, I don't want to hear stories where nothing happened,' he resumed, his piercing gaze directed at the screen. 'You've been away for weeks – is that all you've got for me?'

'There's only one story worth telling these days,' a plump, bald man who had taken a seat on the stool to my left interrupted. Harry handed him a beer bottle through the railings. He took a long slug.

'Now that's a story.' Harry's jowls wobbled as he nodded his approval.

'You've heard it?' the man said. The striplight above us was reflected like a halo in the dark skin of his scalp. I had seen him in the bar before, but we'd never exchanged more than a greeting.

3

With his round, shiny face and bulging eyes, fixed like Harry's on the TV, he had the look of a newly-anointed baby.

'I've heard bits of it,' Harry said. 'Nobody's told me the whole thing. The bar's been dead since I got back. You two are the first customers I've had in days.'

'Yeah, everyone's run out of money,' the man replied.

'You know the whole story?' Harry looked round at him. 'Been skipping church again have you?'

'Everyone's been skipping church,' the man said with a grin, taking another gulp of beer. 'They all came to worship in here instead.'

Darkness had fallen, bringing with it the usual swarm of mosquitoes, but apart from a pair of waitresses slouched snoozing in plastic chairs, the seating area behind us was empty. Harry's bar, The Dashiki Inn, was a spacious affair. Its walls, daubed inside and out with the primary colours of the Warthog beer company logo, stopped short of the steeply thatched roof to allow the warm air to flow through. A network of randomly-placed wooden pole fences suggested an attempt at a Wild West effect. On the music system in one corner, powered by the bar's generator (the island no longer had mains electricity), American pop music was playing quietly to the empty dancefloor.

'I haven't heard the story,' I said. 'What happened?' On the ferry I'd heard some feverish chatter about a mysterious beauty, but none of my fellow passengers knew anything concrete.

The churchman fiddled with a safety pin attached to the hood of his jacket, a brown parka lined with fake fur that must once have adorned an overweight European. 'What are you going to give me for it?' he asked with a smirk.

'You can have some chicken if you like.' I had bought a live chicken from a fellow passenger on the boat and taken it to Harry's kitchen to be beheaded and fried.

4

'Yeah I'll have some chicken,' the churchman said. 'And get me five skewers of goat, too.' He clicked his fingers at one of the waitresses, who woke with a start and sloped off to the kitchen.

'So you want to know about the girl?' he said.

'Why not?' I replied, intrigued.

He drained his beer. 'What about you, Harry? You want to hear it too don't you? What are you going to give me?'

'Here, have another beer,' Harry said, 'but it'd better be good.'

The man turned towards me on his stool, clutching by the neck his bottle of warm Warthog. His bloated eyes had come alive, and as he looked at me for the first time I saw in them an ardour that suggested the sacrifice of a limb of my chicken might not be wasted.

'She came from far away in the south,' he boomed in a voice of sudden loudness. 'She arrived one evening, a Monday I think it was. There was nobody in here, just me and the girls. I was drinking a beer, watching TV. Football I think. Yeah, Monday night football. I saw her coming in out of the corner of my eye. As soon as she came through the door my hand started shaking. And I mean really shaking, not just quivering like it does when I've had too much to drink the night before. The beer was sloshing out of the neck like a premature ejaculation. You know I never put a bottle down unless it's empty, Harry. Well I had to put this one down or it would've emptied itself. Even the girls couldn't keep their eyes off her, and it wasn't just the usual staring at newcomers - for a moment they even turned away from the TV.'

His eyes were burning me with their fire. Big beads of sweat were breaking out like smallpox on his scalp. He finished his beer and I ordered us both another, topping up mine with a fresh sachet of sugar cane gin.

'What did she look like then?' Harry asked. He too had turned from the screen. His eyes were fixed on the storyteller.

The churchman took a breath, as if beginning a sermon. 'I've never seen such beauty,' he said. 'And I'm from Africa, where we still have real beauty, where we haven't destroyed it all. I don't mean your manufactured beauty you have in Europe, your paintings and buildings and all that stuff. I mean natural beauty, the beauty God wanted us to see.'

I thought about arguing, but wanted him to get to the point. 'Anyway, the girl?' I said.

'Yeah get on with it,' said Harry.

The churchman raised the beer bottle to his lips, but lowered it without drinking. 'She was the most beautiful I've ever seen,' he said.

'You told us that already,' Harry jeered. 'What was so great about her?'

'Where do I start?' he said. I shifted in my seat. 'Her ankles –'

'Her ankles!' Harry was growing impatient. 'Who cares about her bloody ankles?'

'Her ankles,' the churchman went on, 'were the most graceful that ever floated over the earth. They were as light as wisps of smoke from a cooking fire. In the days when we still cooked with wood, I mean, not kerosene. When the smell of the firewood soothed you like those silver things the Ethiopians swing around in their churches.' He paused, contemplating. 'In the days when there was still wood to cook with,' he added. 'Africa is losing its beauty too, you know.'

'That's more like it,' said Harry, rolling his lips in approval. 'What about the rest of her? Was her rump nice and jaunty? Were her thighs firm and plump?' We had been joined at the bar by three young men in football shirts. They were watching the wrestling, and passing round a Monastery cigarette. They ordered a beer to share, and Harry set three glasses before them. At a shout from the kitchen one of the waitresses trudged off to fetch our fried chicken. The cook had glazed it in ginger and scattered a few chips on the plate between the bird and the churchman's charred goat kebabs. The girl poured water on our hands from a pitcher and we scrubbed them over a plastic bowl with a crumbling lump of soap. The churchman plucked at the meat with his fingers while I struggled with the flimsy, Chinese-made cutlery. Chomping on the tough flesh, he motioned to Harry to replace his empty beer bottle. Still chewing, he went on:

'Her skin. It was unblemished, as flawless as a diamond in a West African rainforest stream.' He paused again. 'In the days when West Africa still *had* diamonds,' he clarified. 'The days when it still had rainforest.' Behind us the waitresses gasped as a wrestler cascaded from a great height onto his prone rival.

'So she had nice skin on her ankles,' Harry said. 'Is that all you've got for us?'

'No, far from it,' the churchman said with a smile. 'I haven't told you about her eyes yet.'

'Oh, her eyes,' the young men in football shirts swooned in unison. Once they'd realised what we were talking about they had moved nearer, and were no longer looking at the TV. They had only sipped at their beer. 'Her eyes were like nothing in heaven or earth,' one of them said. 'Even Africa has never seen such beauty. They were so deep yet so bright. And the watery film that covered them - it shone like tears.' The boy's friends murmured in agreement. The cigarette between his fingers had burned down to the filter.

'Exactly,' the churchman said, pushing out his lower lip and nodding. He had finished his kebabs and most of my chicken and was looking satisfied.

'A film of tears,' Harry repeated. 'Very poetic.' He turned to the churchman, ignoring his signal for another beer. 'But if she was so great, the loveliest thing ever to walk the land and all that, what the hell was she doing here?'

The churchman shrugged. 'She came for the fishermen I suppose, like all the other girls.'

'But the fishermen are finished,' Harry said. 'And there aren't any other girls anymore. Sounds to me like she's a bit behind the times. What was she like in bed? Did you have to ask her parents for her hand in marriage before you could give her one?'

'I've no idea. Nobody took her to bed. She wanted thirty thousand a go.'

'Thirty thousand?' Harry spluttered. 'Here? Nobody's got two thousand, let alone thirty. Look at these girls.' He pointed at the waitresses, who had been joined at their table by three other women. 'Hardly fighting off the customers are they, and you can have one of them for a thousand on a quiet night.' He shook his head and poured himself a gin. 'Thirty thousand. My God.'

'You did all right though, eh Harry?' the man said. 'This place was full every night. I see you've got yourself a new TV with the proceeds.' On the screen, a wrestler was banging a rival's unbloodied head against a corner stanchion.

'It was better than usual,' Harry admitted. 'Most people still only bought one drink a night though. So she left because no one could afford her? Why didn't she drop her price?'

'There was one who could afford her. Old Balty's still got some money hidden away.'

'Yeah, and the mad old crook doesn't want us to forget it.' They were talking about an islander named Balthazar, once a powerful politician in the lake region who had reputedly lost his mind and most of his fortune after being cursed by a witch. Now a lonely old man with delusions of influence, Balty had entered Harry's bar brandishing thirty crisp thousand-shilling notes.

'But that night she was sick,' the churchman went on. 'The other girls said it was women's problems or something. More likely he was too old and ugly for her. The next day she was gone.'

'That's it?' said Harry.

'That's all I know.'

'I gave you a beer for that? I knew most of that already.'

But while Harry was outraged, I was pensive. Admittedly I was feeling lightheaded by now after one too many beer and gin cocktails, but the girl's story, and in particular the unprecedented fee she charged, had aroused my curiosity.

And it wasn't just the men who talked about her. Leaving Harry and the churchman arguing about whether the story had merited a free drink, I slid off my stool and pulled a plastic chair over to the waitresses' table. The waitresses were staring at their phones. The women who had joined them were watching the TV, on which blonde female wrestlers in bikinis were pulling each other's hair and snarling. The two younger women were as lithe as eels, their tight, breast-hugging white vests throwing their nipples into rugged relief. With them sat Madame E., older and more elegant in a floor-length green and gold dress, the words 'Love Conquers All' tattooed on her left forearm. Once beautiful, with a wide forehead, brilliant green eyes, and a small, soft mouth, her years on the island had weathered her. Her old dream of flying to South Africa to audition for a reality TV show – she had come here to save for the plane ticket – had faded with her looks. Although she insisted that her plan would soon come to fruition, the glassy look in her eyes betrayed her knowledge that after so long stagnating on the lake, her age (and the fact that her willingness to have live televised sex with her housemates was no longer a source of competitive advantage) ruled her out of consideration.

I ordered a round of beers, for old times' sake. Business, they said, was terrible. Things had been bad enough before the girl had arrived; now, with all the islanders' cash spent on journeying to see her, the industry was in its death throes. At first, Madame E. told me, the other women had resented the new arrival's beauty, and her monopoly over the men's attention. Most had shunned her, some had insulted her, one or two had tried to assault her (Harry's brother, who had been looking after the bar while he was away, had had to hold them back). Through it all, Madame E. reported, the girl had remained calm and dignified. 'She never got angry with them,' she said. 'She just took it. She understood.'

Eventually a few men resorted to the cheaper women to relieve their frustration. Madame E., who had expected this expensive new entrant to the market to be arrogant and aloof, was surprised by the girl's kindness. She was happy to look after the other women's children while they were working, and brave in defending them when drunk clients harassed them or refused to pay. 'She sang so beautifully to the babies that they just drifted softly into sleep. She was as gentle as snowflakes coming to rest on Mount Kilimanjaro.' Madame E. paused. 'When there *was* snow on Kilimanjaro. I suppose we didn't want to like her, but we couldn't help it. All of us cried when she left.' She slapped at a mosquito on her left forearm, but it flew up towards the light. The waitresses were taking pictures of themselves with their phones.

One of the younger girls had moved her chair closer to mine. Under the table, as Madame E. talked, she was rubbing her bare foot up and down my leg. She was beautiful like all the others, with fresh-looking skin, shiny, straightened hair and voluptuous painted lips, but although I was now quite drunk I was unusually unmoved by her advances. My mind was filled with thoughts of the thirty-thousand-shilling girl. Anyone who could charge so much more than her competitors, I'd concluded, must be a different calibre of courtesan. I had decided in my alcoholic haze that I had to see her, and when Madame E.'s companion lifted her thigh onto mine and coiled her ankle softly around my calf, instead of responding I held my leg steadfastly still.

The churchman came over. 'I wanted to talk to you about something, Hodge,' he said, leering as he looked down at our entwined limbs, 'before you retire for the evening.'

The girl put her hand between her thigh and the hem of my shorts. 'I'm planning to visit the Emirates,' the man said. 'Can you write me an invitation letter to help me get a visa?'

I'd fielded similar requests more times than the Home Office, and would have been locked up for running a people-trafficking racket if I'd acceded to a small fraction of them (nor was this the first time I'd been mistaken for an Arab – when African children received no response to their enthusiastic "White Man" shouts they would often try "Indian", "Arab" or, these days, "Chinaman" next).

'Sorry, I can't help you,' I said, relieved. 'I'm from England.'

He looked incredulous. 'Yeah I know. That's where I want to go, where the greatest team in the world plays. Now that's real European beauty.'

He was referring to a football stadium sponsored by an Arab airline (nobody knew if it had a real name – it had been called the Emirates Stadium from the day it opened). The girl was tickling the flabby inside of my thigh and staring at my lips as I spoke. Reasoning that since everyone is selling something it would be churlish not to allow her an opportunity to hone her marketing skills, I let her get on with it.

'I don't live in England anymore,' I explained to the man, unsure whether this mattered. 'You have to be living there to be able to invite someone. Maybe if I go back one day...'

He asked for my phone number, and in the manner of any African dealing with a supplicant I gave him the number of a SIM card I seldom used. Beckoning the other young girl to follow him, he made for the exit.

The beer was eroding my resolve. The girl was still gazing at my lips – a trick she must have learned from films - while I talked increasingly slurred nonsense to her. Finally she pulled me outside and, in an alley strewn like a jellyfish die-off with used condoms, leaned back against the wood-slatted wall of what was once a DVD shack. As I peeled her black leggings down her glistening brown thighs she began to whimper with pleasure. She wrapped her legs around me, her body feather-light against the rattling plywood slats. Her moans altered neither in tone, rhythm nor volume until, a few minutes later, I added my own passion fruit-flavoured scabbard to the rubbery sea at our feet.

2

I stayed on the island for a while, picking up scraps of information about the girl, scrutinising the few photographs that had been taken of her, and listening to the islanders' paeans to her beauty and purity of character. I was still on gardening leave from the charity I'd worked for, and my freelance project on the island had done well enough that I was no longer needed to run it. I had time on my hands, and plenty of thirty thousands to spend.

The aid industry had been a boon to my finances. Living on a European wage in a poor, cheap country, it was difficult to spend more than a tiny proportion of your income. Most aid workers had the greater part of their salaries paid into bank accounts back home, and they quickly amassed enough savings to get on the property ladder, build up a pension fund and, later, to send their kids to international schools to snort cocaine with the spawn of politicians. I had no children, property or pension, but my running costs were higher than most and I had kept my money with me. Although I hadn't managed to spend all of it, I had nonetheless attained a quality of life I couldn't have dreamed of if I'd stayed in England.

Nor were the attractions of humanitarian work as a career choice limited to the economic. Some of my peers had become aid workers for the glamour, the kudos of toughing it out in dangerous environments while their friends languished in grey offices. Others were lured by the glory, the halo their work conferred on them when they went home for Christmas. Some had gone into the industry in rebellion against their comfortable middle-class backgrounds, or because a stint overseas would look good on their CV once the time came to get a real job. Most were drawn, too, by the colonial lifestyle – the sundowners on the verandah, the tennis or yacht club membership, the help around the house, the year-round tan.

My own motivations were more expansive. University had not lived up to its promise, and my first objective on leaving had been to emigrate. Potbellies being unfashionable among the sultry left-wing girls with whom I'd shared the halls of the school of modern languages, I had been left to try my luck with less fastidious sorts from the veterinary and dentistry departments. Such is the exaltation of skinniness these days that even this took a great deal of hard work (weeks of sweet talk, showers of gifts, ignominies of self-abasing cajolery), and I emerged from the British education system in need of softer targets.

I started off in food, doling out emergency rations for one of the big nutrition charities (or NGOs, as they call themselves to avoid sounding paternalistic). The timing of my arrival in Africa was propitious, for it coincided with an upsurge in the number of local people employed in the industry. Like all big international NGOs, mine was run by white people, and white people filled all the senior positions. Nowadays, however, whites-only employment policies have gone out of fashion. They don't look good. Nor can you employ locals only as tea boys or punkah-wallahs, which even your naivest funder will realise is tokenism. These days you have to have non-white faces in more prominent positions - on the frontlines for media visibility, and in the offices in the capital for when foreign donors visit (there are exceptions to this rule - you could have had an officeful of Ku Klux Klansmen in hoods when delegations from one recent US administration were visiting and nobody would have noticed).

But this new spirit of equality, diversity and inclusion (or EDI as it was known in acronym-loving foreign aid circles) had limits. For although you now had to employ local people, you barely had to pay them. Local staff received only a fraction of what imported staff were paid for doing the same job. It would have taken your average African food parcel hurler nearly a year to earn what I was taking home every month. This was common practice in the international NGO world. A twelfth of my salary, it was reasoned, was an unimaginably fantastic sum for most Africans. Everybody wanted to work for an international NGO – all the best-educated people begged, bribed and fought for the most menial of jobs. Why offer more?

And the disparity in wealth didn't end with the respective salaries. It was stretched yet wider by the gulf in outgoings. Expatriate aid workers received perks on top of their wages. Many had their rent paid (one of the reasons rental prices in African cities are higher than those in London). They were given Land Cruisers, private health insurance, laptops and smartphones. Every year there was a free flight home. The only things they had to cough up for out of their own pockets were food, alcohol and leisure activities. They – we – were awash with cash.

Local employees, on the other hand, enjoyed none of these benefits. They had to catch public transport to work, rent their own homes (often in slums or distant suburbs considered too dangerous for Westerners), and sort out their own healthcare (more robust to tropical diseases, they didn't need to go private). On top of all this they had to make regular and substantial handouts to relatives, friends and neighbours, who on hearing they had landed such a lucrative job would demand their share of its fruits. Those who shirked this duty would be permanently banished from their communities. Even in these times, few Africans could countenance such ostracism, and after paying off the queues of supplicants they were left with little in the way of surplus funds.

To the NGO's female staff, therefore, I was a godsend. Sleeping with those unfortunates the organisation euphemistically called its "clients" was forbidden (humanitarians caught demanding sex from famine victims in return for food were fired on the spot), but liaisons with locally-engaged women were tolerated as beneficial to all parties. In Africa I didn't need the sultry socialists from the school of modern languages, most of whom had ended up here too, and their surprise that I of the crassly-bloated paunch was standing in the same trucks as them, lobbing food parcels into the same grateful outstretched arms, soon gave way to self-righteous consternation as I began a series of liaisons with their locally-appointed colleagues.

3

My rootling around the island proved less productive than I had hoped, and I learned little beyond what the churchman had told me. Nobody could tell me why the girl had gone there or why she had left, let alone why she charged such an exorbitant fee. They did know, however, where she had left for, and after a few days listening to the aching eulogies of the normally-brusque islanders, I packed my bag and headed to the jetty to board the early-morning ferry to the mainland.

The town of Itongo lay three hundred miles to the west of the lake in the central African forests. It was a diamond centre. I had spent a week there several years earlier, soon after the outbreak of the war which had flushed in thousands of refugees from the surrounding jungle. It had been a nondescript but bustling place, with Hummers and Land Cruisers clogging a single main avenue lined with Lebanese diamond dealerships. My colleagues and I had handed out food parcels and peanut paste sachets to starving kids, but when one of the dozen rebel armies that was fighting in the vicinity threatened to kidnap foreigners it became too dangerous for us to stay. Now the rebels had either been eliminated by mercenaries or bribed to join the government side, and the town was peaceful. As the only place within five hundred miles whose inhabitants might be able to afford the girl's fee, Harry's brother and the other girls had not been surprised when she'd asked them how to get there.

The ferry to the mainland, a rusting, British-built affair that had been plying these waters since the 1950s, was crammed with passengers. The lounge below the bridge was full, its occupants undeterred by being forced to watch videos showing happy choristers singing hymns at full volume. To avoid spending the six-hour journey on my feet I secured a patch of metal floor on the lower deck outside. I had on my wide-brimmed straw sunhat, a long-sleeved white shirt that had seen better days, and my white shorts. After slapping suncream on my legs, I leaned back against my holdall to sleep off the hangover I'd acquired in Harry's the previous evening.

Within minutes I was woken by a knee pushing at my shoulder. Looking up, I saw the corpulent figure of a man who kept a café in the island's main market. He was nudging me aside so that a porter could put down a stack of empty beer crates. A second porter dumped a pile of wooden boxes beside the crates. The man had served me lunch in his café one day, and had offered his catering services for my nutrition project (I had prolonged my stay on the lake by persuading five middle-aged British Rotary Club members who had grown rich in the interior design boom to fund a food distribution campaign to help battle the latest drought). The caterer had promised me a free meal every day if I awarded him the contract to supply the project, but following a violent bout of food poisoning after feasting on his beef kebabs I rejected his offer. The Rotarians came to the island every year to paint walls in clinics and schools, announcing their arrival by parading down the main street on motorbike-taxis as newly-unemployed local wall painters looked on helplessly. It would not have done for the returning heroes to be associated with wiping out hordes of hungry islanders.

'Don't yawn Hodge,' the man said, looking down at me. 'You'll let the devil in.'

'I think he's already ensconced,' I replied, my attempt to stretch stifled by his crates.

He paid his porters and took a seat beside me on one of the wooden boxes. He was dressed in fake American jeans and a grey shirt that showed off his beer belly. His eyes were scurrying and shrewd, and his face had the hard, wide-cheekboned look common to many of the islanders. 'Your breath smells terrible,' he said, frowning. 'Are you drunk?'

'None of your business,' I growled, feeling nauseous. 'First you push me out of my seat, then you insult me.'

'I'm just letting you know,' he said. 'You might want to have a wash or something. Here, have another beer.' It was eight in the morning, but I took the bottle he proffered.

A pied crow landed on the stack of beer crates and squawked. Black kites wheeled overhead, shrieking. The boat's engine had not yet been fired up, the scheduled departure time long past. I had assumed the man was going to the lakeshore to stock up for his café, and was surprised when he told me he was going to the capital.

'I'm doing the catering for the police banquet,' he explained. The president had fired an unusually zealous anti-corruption czar, and police stations across the country were holding lavish parties to celebrate. 'I'm going to the new shopping mall to buy provisions.'

'The new shopping mall?'

'Yes, the Temple! You don't know about it?' He laughed at my ignorance. 'It's the biggest mall in East Africa. And the best – all the famous stores are there. It's got fifteen cafés with fully qualified baristas, half a dozen cupcake shops, a store that sells more than fifty types of pasta, and kitchen places selling all the latest inventions from America and China. And they've given me enough money to buy the most expensive food and wine in the mall. More than enough, in fact. I'll have a little spare to stock up my own larder as well.'

18

'Why all the empty crates?' I said.

'They'll charge more if they have to provide the boxes,' he replied, not yet accustomed to non-African retail practices. 'They wouldn't trust me to return them.'

'And why are you going all the way to the capital for it?' an old man in a trilby hat interrupted. He was sitting near us on a battered attaché case, his hands clasped on his knees. 'You could buy what you need in Itongo in the markets.'

'Itongo!' the caterer exclaimed. 'The police haven't hired me to go shopping in Itongo! They don't just want a kilo of beans and a bag of rice, you know. They want the best that money can buy. And they want it nicely packaged too – they don't want market sacks.'

The old man chuckled. 'They want those old boxes, do they?' he said.

'These are for transport,' the man replied. 'They won't see them at the banquet. They'll see the sculpted wine bottles, the finely-sliced cold meats and cheeses, and the extravagantly-decorated cakes. They've given me enough money to pay someone to do the design work. It'll be a feast not just for the stomach but for the eyes.'

The engine sputtered into life and the captain sounded the horn. Latecomers were scurrying down the landing stage by the crumbling customs house, waving at the boat to wait. When all were aboard we moved off. On the deck, people had kicked off their flip-flops and were sitting in little groups on the floor or on boxes. They were chatting and laughing, unbothered by having to sit jammed up against each other or by having a stranger's snoozing head on their shoulder, shin or lap. I looked on as people who had never met talked as if they'd been friends for decades, as men slapped hands to congratulate one another's wit, and as women in boldly-coloured skirts and headscarves sympathised with problems or celebrated successes.

The ferry made stately progress, its engine spewing clouds of black smoke above our heads. The caterer and the old man were talking about the girl. 'The arch of her back...' the caterer was saying as he contemplated the island's receding hills. 'It was as perfectly curved as the horn of the black rhino. Before the horns were hacked off, that is, and turned into medicine for impotent Asians. In the days when we still *had* black rhinos.'

The old man nodded. 'And her eyes,' he added quietly. 'Those tears that never fell. Only your stomach fell when you saw them.' He took off his trilby as if speaking of the dead.

Three young women were sitting near us. They wore jeans under their wraparound skirts, their wigs gleaming in the sunlight. I had seen them before, working the bars of one of the smaller islands and now and again in Harry's. Overhearing the conversation, one of them, a tall, Nilotic beauty whose red lipstick stood out like a stop-light against her dark skin, joined in:

'She wasn't just beautiful,' she said, 'she was a good person. We wanted to hate her – she took all our clients away from us. But she couldn't help that. She thought we might get more business, not less, because of all the men coming to see her.'

'Maybe that's why she left,' another girl said. 'She felt bad about it. I was sad she went though. She was a good friend to us.'

'And so generous with the food they gave her,' said the Nilotic girl, who must have been of Sudanese or Somali descent. 'She ate hardly any of it herself.'

'Yes, Harry did all right out of her,' the caterer laughed. 'He's never had it so good.'

'Some of us did OK too once the fishermen's patience wore out,' the third girl said. 'But that's it now - the islands are finished. We're going home.'

I took a curative slug of beer and stood to stretch my legs. I picked my way over to the railing, where two young men in sunglasses and outsize headphones were tapping on the screens of their smartphones. I wondered if they might be writing messages to each other, but they were standing so close together that I discarded the idea as preposterous.

I leant against the railing and watched the lake. If you looked straight ahead, to the hard line of the horizon where the sun-stippled water met the pale morning sky, you could imagine this vast body of water which had for so long sustained the millions living around it as pure and life-giving. Only close to the boat could you see the patches of off-white scum, the floating snails that carried the slow-killing bilharzia parasite, and the vast green clouds of algae that had turned the lake into a toxic pea soup.

For a few years there had been a fishing boom here. Airports had sprung up on the shore so that perch and tilapia could be exported to fished-out Europe and Asia. Unmarked cargo planes took fish from the lake and brought weapons in, to feed the war around Itongo. Western development agencies, eager to jump on a winning horse, pumped in billions of dollars to build fishing ports, processing factories and markets.

But the lessons of Europe and Asia had not been learned. Tens of thousands of new vessels took to the water, carrying hundreds of thousands of fishermen. Local politicians, the boom's main beneficiaries, imported trawlers, which cleared the lakebed of life. Pollution from the factories, its path cleared by bribery, streamed into the lake, killing off the fish that had dodged the trawlers' dragnets. Catch sizes plummeted. The industry collapsed. Now only the most desperate still plied their trade here, foraging forlornly for the few remaining fish. For miles in all directions around the ferry there was not a single boat. Even the prostitutes were jumping ship.

I climbed back to my bag and fell asleep. The caterer woke me as we reached port in the lakeside city. The shore was lined with defunct fish processing factories, their gates, doors and signboards plundered by looters. Below them in the shallows children splashed and washed in a green scum studded with syringes and plastic water bottles. Near the dock I boarded a minibus for the eight-hour ride to Itongo. A drunk crammed in next to me handed me a stick of sugarcane to chew.

4

The picture of Itongo that was preserved in my memory was no longer a useful guide. The place was a shell. On the town's main avenue, its tarmac cratered with potholes, barely a shop or tea shack lay intact. Walls that had not collapsed were pockmarked with bullet holes. Doors and tin roofs had been looted, every window smashed. The surrounding bush had taken advantage of the desolation and crept back in, seeding the abandoned Lebanese bungalows with foliage and infusing the alleys between them with its silence.

Only in the backstreets, the residents perhaps fearful of being too visible, were there signs of human life. The town's drinking joints seemed unpromising targets for a top-end prostitute, but I had heard that one or two of the diamond mines on the outskirts had resumed operations since the end of the war, and I knew that a number of the women who had given up on the lake had made their way here.

I was diligent in my search for the girl. Day and night in the muggy heat I traipsed around the bars and guest houses. Suspecting that they might be concealing her whereabouts out of professional jealousy, I bought dozens of drinks for the town's working girls, but the tongue-loosening effect of the alcohol made no difference. None of them had seen her, and I drew a blank too with the miners who returned to Itongo's watering holes in the evenings.

Slowly, the drinking, the wheedling, the heat and the humidity combined to sap my strength, and for solace I resumed a relationship with a girl I'd known on the island. This only compounded my exhaustion, not just through the physical exertion of the daily romps in my guesthouse bedroom, but by leaving the mattress so sodden that to get any sleep at night I had to lie on the concrete floor, which my aching back could tolerate only until the small hours.

Ever since I had arrived in Africa I'd made a point of giving business to its working girls. I couldn't think of a strong reason to desist, and it seemed a good way of doing my bit for the local economy ("trade, not aid", as the international development consultants' mantra went). My security guards would watch with impotent envy as what they called my revolving door sucked in and spat out a parade of young bodies. Added to the steady flow of locally-engaged staff, these professionals had made my early years on the continent a writhing fettucine of debauchery.

And it wasn't just the quantity; the quality was first-rate, too. In Africa there was none of the Catholic guilt so common back home, none of the frigidity or affected cool. Here the girls cut loose. They'd do anything you wanted, and when you ran out of ideas they'd come up with fresh projects of their own. Often they would give me more than I'd bargained for, pounding away late into the night until they'd wrung my loins of everything they had.

Were the sultry socialists jealous? Not of me – they regarded me with even more scorn now than they had at university – but of my lack of inhibition with local women. As I walked off after a hard day's parcel-throwing with a smiling beauty on my arm they would look on po-faced. The next morning they would whisper among themselves as we climbed, late and sated, into the truck. Eventually, after orgies of soul-searching, most of them succumbed to the temptation too. Those who had come out with white boyfriends split up with them after a few months. Lovers left back home were lucky to last a fortnight. Although they might not have gone into the industry for the sex, it was often the sex that kept them there.

You will perhaps (but who can be sure of people's standards these days?) consider me exploitative. On many counts I admit the charge. My wealth gave me pulling power, and while the sultry socialists saw my paunch as a symbol of my shamelessness, for African girls it bespoke success and money. But in my defence I would argue that there are grades of exploitation – we're all exploited by someone. And if it hadn't been me exploiting the girls, it would have been someone else, someone who on the balance of probabilities would have treated them a good deal less chivalrously than I did.

Consider the alternatives - and before you accuse me of stereotyping, I've talked about this to women all over Africa. I've talked to full-time professionals, to part-timers, to girls who wouldn't regard themselves as prostitutes at all. And I mean talked – I'm not one of those men who just dips in and out with no effort to get to know them. You can rest assured my research sample is robust.

As an ordinary African girl beginning your copulatory career, your staple diet is likely to consist of impoverished African men. Neighbours, schoolmates, people you meet in a bar or at the mosque, these men are generally harmless, frequently too drunk to perform. They are also, however, penniless. They have no spare cash. It doesn't matter whether the relationship is professional or permanent: they will never be able to give you more than basic sustenance.

If you aspire to better things - to hair extensions, skin whitener, high heels, a smartphone – you need to raise your sights. You need a man with money. Mostly this means a man who is at best amoral, at worst an enthusiastic criminal. For there are no clean fortunes in Africa. Either you're white and you piled up your loot on the buckled backs of slaves, or you're black and you stole it from your compatriots once the whites left. A girl looking to move up in the world, to be whisked away to a life of modern convenience, must play a dangerous game. Targeting men with money doesn't mean you will score a man with money - other girls have the same goal, and competition is fierce. But if you do strike lucky, how you will be treated is a crap shoot.

Look at the options. In southern Africa your best hope of a big payday is a mining magnate, a mercenary or an arms dealer. These men will be cold and businesslike - not much fun but good payers, emotionally undemanding and only occasionally lethal. Warlords – ambitious West Africans who have chosen the traditional route to their countries' treasures – are less predictable. They will either treat you like a princess or drug you up as a sex slave. In East Africa your best prospect is a politician or one of his business associates, newly minted on mineral wealth after bribing their way to power. This sort is no different to the *nouveaux riches* anywhere. He will show off to his cronies by paying you more than you ask, but if you want to avoid a beating or worse, you'd better make your groans of ecstasy loud enough for them to hear.

And then there are the whites (Lebanese and Indians tend to stick to their own women, and like everybody else I know nothing about the Chinese). I don't mean white Africans, wistful old colonials so terrified of contaminating their tiny gene pool that they will risk only the occasional dalliance. I mean non-African whites, from Europe and North America - if not NGO workers, then diplomats, tourists, missionaries, businessmen or visiting politicians. The sex won't be great (even after you've got past their initial anthropological curiosity), but nor will it exhaust you, and the white man's assiduous condom use means you're unlikely to contract any new diseases. Many of these types will want to help

26

you in some way, materially with trinkets and cash, emotionally by consoling you for your plight, being your friend. Some will even reciprocate your foreplay. The shrewder girls play along with all this, for a white man, unlike all their other options, can mean hitting the jackpot. These men are a long way from home, lonely, and used to relationships that last more than five minutes. A few will want to see you more than once. One or two are in the market for a serious relationship – a shared home with light bulbs and running water, a regular clothing allowance, a retinue of servants, and, one day, a passport to the land of milk and honey.

As a member of this last group, therefore, I was one of an African girl's better bets. And they knew it. Whenever a white man appeared in a nightclub or a bar he was swamped. The sexiest girls in the joint would fight, sometimes with fists, for his attention. And as I say, I didn't just dip in and out – I would talk to them first, find out about their lives, buy them a few drinks or a meal. With me they were not only safer than they would have been with most other men; they were pampered too. This girl, the one I had known on the lake, was no exception. When she saw me walk into the bar in Itongo she was delighted. Back on the island she had told me I was different to the rest. In my asthmatic lovemaking she saw tenderness, in my lapping between her legs romance. It was not your ordinary client-prostitute relationship. I was pleased to see her, too.

In rekindling this old flame, however, I didn't forget why I was here – my friend from the island was a generous sparring partner, but I was convinced by now that the thirty-thousand-shilling girl must be in a different realm of artistry. For days between debauches I trawled the grimy streets, but in my search for information I was getting nowhere. Realising I might be more likely to find her in a place whose economy hadn't caved in than in these ghost towns, I was on the point of moving on. Then, one evening, I got a lead.

I was sitting with my young escort in the leafy garden of a liquor store. In the days before the war had reached Itongo the place had been bustling and noisy, with Congolese bands playing lilting tunes to rowdy crowds of diamond miners. Now it was quiet, just us and a couple of men silently drinking beer with their women. I had begun to tell the girl of my plans to continue my search elsewhere when two men walked in and made for the far end of the garden. One was tall and lanky in a grey cape coated with dust, the other younger and fresher of face. They took seats at a table under a mango tree, and a waitress brought them ginger ales.

I hadn't come across these men during my wanderings around the town, so I asked the girl about them. 'He's a gentleman,' she said, returning the tall man's wave. I raised my eyebrows. 'No, really,' she protested. 'He's not interested in sex. He talks to us like a gentleman, he's very kind. He had a wife – that's his son with him – and he's devoted to her memory. Look at him, he doesn't even drink. He's a good Christian.'

I looked over at the man. His face, like his body, was long and thin, his gaunt cheeks giving him a sorrowful look. 'What's he doing here?' I asked the girl. 'Mining?' She nodded. 'He's looking for a site to mine,' she said. 'Before that he was a warlord.'

Her expression on dropping this bombshell didn't change, but I was unable to stop myself spluttering on my mouthful of Warthog. 'A warlord and a gentleman?' I said once I'd regained my composure. 'He's very polite,' she replied, 'If you talk to him you won't believe he's fought in so many battles.'

'He certainly looks like he's seen a few things,' I said. 'His son looks happy though.' Where the father's skin was worn and dry, the younger man's was shiny, his face childishly puffy. He wore long dreadlocks and a red, black and white patchwork jacket. The father's expression as they talked was glum, the son's bright and animated.

'He was just a child during the war,' the girl said. 'He has blood on his hands too, but it had a different effect on him.'

I asked her why I hadn't seen them before.

'I told you, they're looking for somewhere to mine. They've been here a few weeks but they move around – they don't often come to town.'

'Will he talk to me?' I asked - if they had been roaming the district they might have news of the girl.

'Of course he will. He's polite to everyone. Come on, I'll introduce you.'

We walked over and the warlord stood to pull out a chair for the girl. He shook my hand solemnly as we took seats around the plastic table.

I was unsure how to begin. I had never met a warlord before, and while I must have met child soldiers, it had been difficult while dishing out food parcels to distinguish them from other children. I was relieved when the younger man broke the silence. 'You're looking for diamonds,' he said, his voice high-pitched and singsong. I replied that that wasn't what had brought me here, but to keep the conversation going I asked if he had any.

'We haven't started mining yet,' he said. 'But if you give me your number I can let you know when we do.'

It was proving difficult to find a suitable site, he told me. 'In the old days you would see diamonds by the roadside, but now you have to dig deep or dredge the rivers to find them. You need heavy machinery for that, and even then there's a good chance you won't unearth anything.'

I asked if they had any heavy machinery. 'Not yet,' he replied. 'But we have capital, so we can get it once we find a good place to mine.' He changed the subject: 'Anyway, if diamonds aren't the reason you're here, what is?'

I began to tell them about the girl. No sooner did I mention her than the young man's countenance changed from one of wariness while I was asking about the machinery to one of rapt attention. 'You've seen her?' he said. 'When? What was she doing? Where is she?' Across the table, his father sighed.

I told them I hadn't seen her but was looking for her, and had heard she was in Itongo. The boy shook his head. 'No, she hasn't been here. We saw her on our way here, but that was months ago.'

'Where was that?' I asked, a tremor of excitement at meeting someone who'd seen her quickly snuffed out by the realisation that I was on the wrong track.

'In a village to the east. We were passing through.'

'One evening was all it took,' his father joined in, regarding me sombrely. 'She left the day after we arrived. Two men had had a fistfight over her and she disappeared when she heard about it. But a day was long enough for my son - he fell in love and has hardly slept a wink since.'

'That's true,' the boy admitted. 'But look at me' - he turned to face me - 'even though I don't sleep I'm not tired. My love for her keeps me going. She has healed me, father.'

The old man sucked at his ginger ale through a straw. 'Healed you for now,' he said. 'When you recover from your infatuation we will see if you are still cured.'

On the TV above the liquor store's counter, the contestants of Big Brother Africa were asleep in their beds. My friend was watching them, blank-faced.

'I'll never get over her,' the young man said. 'It's been months since I saw her, yet my love is stronger than ever. I just have to close my eyes and I see her image glittering on the inside of my eyelids. I see her eyelashes, as light as the Amani sunbird's hover, that tiny bird whose last copse of trees our men cut down in the war. And I see her eyes, those eyes that made you tremble to look at them.'

'She was indeed beautiful,' his father admitted with a sorrowful bow of his equine head. 'Her eyes brimmed with tears. They never dried up, but seeing them parched your throat like the harmattan wind of the western deserts.' The boy slammed his hand on the table in agreement, his dreadlocks swaying around his neck. 'And her legs,' the older man went on, momentarily forgetting his reprimand to his son, 'they were as long and graceful as the plucked note of a kora. You will not know about the kora, but it was once, before the ability to play it died out, the source of Africa's most beautiful music.'

His son seemed briefly to swoon, collapsing back into the embrace of his plastic chair. 'My father won't let me go and find her until we've done our penance,' he said, recovering. 'I suppose you know we fought a war here. That's why I was in the rehabilitation centre. That was before we saw the girl. I had to leave – I couldn't stand the other boys' screams at night. My father is taking me on this pilgrimage, but I don't need it now – I'm cured already.'

'Pilgrimage?' I said, unaware of any such scams in this part of Africa. 'Where are you going? Lourdes?'

The older man ignored my snigger. 'Lourdes is where I wanted to go. We are Roman Catholics. That is why we had to fight the war, because our fellows were being persecuted.' In his use of the local tongue he was stiff and formal, making it easy for me to understand him (I had picked up a few words during my previous visit to the area, and thinking the language would be a useful addition to my repertoire had studied it for a while thereafter). 'But the French were on the government's side, not ours. They would arrest us if we went to their country. I know I have committed sins. I regret them, and I know I will be judged for them. But I will be judged by my Lord, not by godless Europeans.'

'Where are you going then?'

'To a great cathedral in the west.'

'It's the biggest in Africa,' the boy said.

'Not just in Africa,' said his father. 'It's the biggest in the whole world. It was not my idea - the nuns who run the rehabilitation centre suggested it.'

31

'That's a very long journey,' I said, guessing which post-independence monstrosity he was talking about.

'We have much to atone for,' he replied. He slipped into confessional mode. He told me about the good cause that had sparked the uprising – the need to put a stop to the repression of his fellow Catholics by an Islamic-fundamentalist government. His acceptance of a leadership role had been reluctant – 'I am a humble lumberjack, not a warrior' - but he couldn't refuse. He said he had been doing God's work, playing his part in defeating the Antichrist and hastening the End of Days.

The only unusual part of his story was his claim that he hated conflict. Most warlords I'd heard about were sadists, who relished the atrocities they inflicted. Their *noms de guerre* were evidence enough – Colonel Castration, Lieutenant Friendly Fires and Brigadier Worst Nightmare had all sown terror during the same war. But this one was different. He contended that he had never had a fight in his life until the war started, and that after every battle he would weep and pray to the spirits of those killed, begging for forgiveness. 'I could not abide the thought of the dead men's spirits wandering restless over the earth,' he told me, gazing at the bottle-top-strewn ground below the table. 'Satan had entered them, it had not been their choosing. They needed to rest, so I pleaded with them for reconciliation. And strange things were happening to my son. I worried that it was the spirits of the departed haunting him and driving him mad.'

A waitress approached us, the soles of her flip-flops scuffing the hard earth, and placed a fresh bottle of ginger beer on the table. The warlord inserted his straw and drank, the insides of his cheeks almost kissing as he sucked. His close-cropped hair was greying, his brow deeply lined. I ordered another Warthog. The night was moonless but clear, the blueblack sky flecked with stars. Over our heads swooped large beige bats, flashing like outsize moths in the dim light emanating from the liquor store. There was nobody else left in the garden.

When the Christian rebels had unseated the Muslim government, the warlord was elated. 'It would mean no more killing,' he said, 'and my son could begin to live a normal life again.' As usual, however, that had not been the end of it. The ruling party had spent its time in power looting the nation's treasures (its members had been so busy stealing that they had neglected to arm themselves against revolt). The rebels had pillaged what remained to fund their campaign. Whole forests had been felled for timber, whole diamond regions emptied. Before the defeated regime's leaders departed for their safe haven in France, they had plundered what was left in the state's coffers. In the government ministries, not a light bulb was spared.

The new government - a snakepit of warlords whose hour of triumph had turned to hair-tearing frustration as they realised there was nothing left in the trough - needed a fresh source of funds to keep the troops and their cronies happy. With no natural resources left to sell off, the obvious solution was foreign aid. The international community had so far ignored the war. It was seen as just another pointless African conflict, and the rich-world public wasn't interested. To capture their attention, creativity would be needed. 'Since I had experience as a lumberjack I was appointed Minister of Forests,' the warlord said. 'But there were few trees still standing, so I had nothing to do. I had plenty of time to think, and finally I came up with an idea.'

The idea, he told me, was for part of the rebel army to break away from the government and declare war on it. Those who headed ministries considered non-essential – the Minister of Tourism, the Minister of Immigration and himself - were chosen to head the new rebel group. But instead of real fighting, this new, staged war would rely on a well-publicised campaign of amputations of civilian limbs. 'We knew the international community would not be able to ignore us anymore if their newspapers were full of severed arms and legs,' he explained. 'Yes, it would be painful for the victims – I knew that and I regretted it. But if we were to get the country back on its feet, sacrifices had to be made.' Through his straw he sucked a jet of ginger ale.

'We kept the amputations to the minimum needed,' he went on, his justification of his actions to an outsider perhaps preparation for a future war crimes trial. 'We started by sending photographs of lepers to the international press, pretending they had been cut with machetes. Then, when there was still no intervention – we later heard that Western governments had been arguing over who would send in troops - we went out into the villages. Many civilians volunteered to be cut. They knew we would not have been able to win the war unless we had had God on our side, and they were keen to help the new Christian government. The peacekeepers arrived soon after. They came from your country - I suppose your leaders saw an opportunity to regain influence here now that the French had gone. The war ended – none of us wanted to lose our lives for a fake war – and the money for reconstruction came pouring in. It was just as we had hoped. We could begin to rebuild our country and we could pay off those warlords who were impatient for recognition for their part in the victory. It did not last, but for a while it seemed our plan had worked.'

It didn't last because once it realised that aid money, which didn't need to be cut down or mined, was an even richer source of plunder than timber or diamonds, the new Christian government split again into factions. This time the revival of the conflict was genuine. The peacekeepers, prohibited from shooting anybody, were impotent to stop a real war, and mercenaries had to be called in from southern Africa to eliminate the main protagonists. By this time the warlord had left the government in disgust. 'It had become a senseless war,' he told me. 'We had started off by defending our people, and had begun to build our New Jerusalem. But Satan had crept back in and taken over the minds of those who had fought so valiantly in God's name. Perhaps all the fighting had weakened them – you need strength to fend off the Devil's temptations.'

I had assumed he was looking for a mine to dig because he needed cash now that he'd left politics, but he claimed it was a philanthropic venture. 'I want to help the children who fought with us in the war. The nuns do a good job of rehabilitating them psychologically, but the children did terrible things, and their communities and families will allow them to return only if they bring money. If they work at a mine they will have something to take with them when they go back to their villages. Once the mine is up and running, we will continue on our pilgrimage.'

At that moment another man came into the bar and approached our table. I was surprised to see a pretty white girl on his arm. The man's face was dark and rugged, his hair close-cropped. He was dressed in the style of a central African dandy, in a tight-fitting lime-green blazer and matching slacks. A silver St Christopher hung from his neck. The girl, who was several inches taller than him, appeared no older than twenty. She wore beige slacks and a light-blue shirt with a designer logo stitched on the pocket. With her wide blue eyes, tied-back blond hair and enthusiastic smile, I took her for a gap-year student.

The warlord introduced the man as his assistant. 'We used to cut trees together and he stayed with me during the war,' he said. 'He has been out looking for a site for us to mine.'

The man shook my hand. 'This is Lucy,' he told me. 'She's from England too.' Lucy's smile grew wider. I asked her what she was doing here. 'I've been volunteering at the rehab centre,' she replied in plummy, Home Counties tones. 'Some of us came out from Buckinghamshire to build a classroom there. Now we've finished it I'm going travelling for a couple of months before I return home.'

The warlord's assistant chuckled. 'These kids think they built the thing themselves,' he said, sticking to the local language, 'but

35

every bit of wall they put up would collapse by the next morning. The inmates had to get up at dawn to fix the mess before the volunteers woke up. They never knew anything about it.' Lucy beamed, uncomprehending. 'She's good at keeping other types of erection upright though,' the man added with a grin, staring at her pert breasts.

'And what's your business here?' he asked me.

'He's looking for the girl,' the boy told him.

'Oh, the girl,' the man said, turning away from his companion. 'The girl whose eyes were as dark as the heart of the African blackwood.' He sighed and shook his head. 'Before we cut them all down. I heard a rumour about her today.'

The boy and I tensed up. 'There's a mine far out in what used to be the forest,' he continued. 'A working mine. They say a pastor's running it.'

'A working mine?' Now the warlord, too, was interested.

'They haven't found much yet,' his assistant said, 'but there are quite a few girls out there.' I glanced at my friend, and knew from her averted gaze that she had kept this information to herself.

'And she's out there too?' the boy demanded, his eyes burning with renewed intensity.

'I met someone who told me she was there, but he hadn't seen her himself.'

I looked at the girl again, and saw resignation in her eyes. I was reluctant to put an end to our afternoon indulgences, but I needed to preserve my energies. It was time to move on.

5

There was no public transport out through the old forest, so I hired a car. The driver was sallow-faced and gruff, and he wore what appeared to be a pair of old jeans wrapped like an oversize bandanna around his head. He spent most of the six-hour journey complaining of the wickedness of Africa's pastors.

'These men are crooks,' his argument went. 'Look at me. I used to wear smart clothes. My skin was clean and young. Then I got a job as a pastor's assistant. I worked for him for seven years and ended up penniless. The money you're paying me is the first I've earned in months.'

His boss, he told me as we lurched through a landscape of abandoned villages and razed forests, was a swindler. Professing alchemical powers bestowed on him by Christ, he had run a scheme in which he used money given to him by his congregation to trade stocks and shares via the internet. God, he told his followers, would reward them for their faith. While the economy was flourishing he had done well, and he convinced his flock to sell off their meagre assets to increase their stakes. When the market turned, however, the scheme collapsed and the pastor, who had skimmed off a percentage of the profits during the good times and risked none of his own money in the bad, fled. The congregants, who couldn't believe that such an esteemed figure would deceive them, came after his assistant, angrily demanding recompense. 'But I'd invested my life savings too,' the poor man complained. 'I had nothing to give them. All I have is this old heap I used to drive the bastard around in. They were running down the street after me as I drove away. They'd have lynched me if they'd got their hands on me.'

We drove on, around us a giant checkers board of tree stumps. The driver pointed out a collapsed river bank, whose demise had buried alive a dozen artisanal miners who had been scouring for diamonds in its lee. 'They're not allowed to mine like that anymore,' he said. 'It all has to follow safety regulations and they have to certify the stones. You'll see when we get to the mine how much notice people are taking of that.'

Eventually the dirt road, whose condition had been deteriorating since we left the town, dribbled away into bush. We pulled up next to a golden Hummer with blacked-out windows. 'That'll be the pastor's,' the driver grumbled. We got out and picked our way along a narrow, sandy track. Thorny scrub scraped at our calves. The early afternoon sun beat down on my straw hat, the only sound the whirr of crickets in the undergrowth. A few yards ahead of us a black snake slithered across the path. The driver, leading the way, stopped to let it pass.

We walked for an hour, my feet squelching in my sweat-soaked sandals. Finally the silence was broken by the faint clink of metal on rock. 'Nearly there,' my companion grunted. I looked around at the ravaged, empty landscape. My prospects of finding the girl here appeared slim.

In the past, I would have considered a place crammed with willing women an attraction in itself. I had been drawn to the island in the lake by the number of working girls who had flocked to it during the fishing boom, and in my early days had taken full advantage of my status as its lone white man. Recently, however, the gloss had come off, and I had found it increasingly difficult to muster the enthusiasm of old.

For Africa was not what it was. When I had first arrived in the continent, some of the women I met had gone to bed with me for pleasure. They enjoyed my company, didn't obviously find me physically repulsive, and were happy – sometimes even eager - for me to take them back to my villa or hotel room at the end of the evening. Although it wasn't easy to tell, since they all made the right noises, some of them seemed to enjoy the sex, too. Many were upset when I broke off the relationship, loitering outside my firmly locked gate while they pleaded with my security guards to let them in. When my protectors stood firm, they would write ardent but illiterate love texts imploring me to reconsider.

Now that world is gone, that innocence no more. I used to think I was rare in my cynicism. At the minor public school I'd attended I had exulted in the nickname Di-Hodgenes, believing in my teenage self-absorption that my sceptical approach to life made me interesting. But these days I'm no more cynical than anyone else. Even in Africa, where for centuries the gullibility of locals gave worldly Europeans free rein to rape and plunder, naivety is a thing of the past. None of the girls is innocent now. None of them does it for pleasure. They do it for cash, or for gifts. Or for cash and gifts. And I'm not just talking about full-time prostitutes here. I'm talking about your average woman, a woman you meet in business class or at a conference. And they want cash up front, not even an initial down payment. They want all of it, 100%. No Credit Offered.

And the sex is lacklustre. They just go through the motions. If it's not you it'll be someone else; there are plenty of men out there, American and Indian, Chinese and African, still a few irrelevant Europeans. If a girl just lies or kneels there and whimpers and gulps at the right time she'll still be giving them more than they're getting in their lonely hotel rooms.

But this girl, I thought, must be different. A thirty-thousand-shilling asking price must mean that she was not just beautiful – plenty of girls in these parts were beautiful – but an outstanding exponent of her craft. However much the islanders eulogised over her looks or the gentleness of her nature, there was no way she could have charged such a high fee without being unusually adroit in bed. She seemed like a throwback, to a time when it wasn't just a race to the bottom, when quality mattered, when people took pride in providing a good service - a time, in short, when you could purchase top-of-the-range sex.

The path stopped at the edge of a deep pit. Men's jeering voices ascended to our ears, followed by laughter at the sight of an overweight white man teetering above them. The pit, a brown scar amid the green of the surrounding scrub, was the size of a football pitch. Dotted along the ledges that ringed its steep terraced walls were two dozen lean young men, barefoot and without helmets, who were burrowing into the layers of rock and mud with pickaxes and spades.

Shouting above the tinkling, my driver asked the men where we might find their boss. They pointed off to one side, and we descended a path that led away from the pit towards a large brown pool. As we neared the pool we heard a voice singing what sounded like hymns. At the water's edge, three half-naked youths, legs submerged to their knees, were bent over bamboo-framed trays that they had placed on the bank. Peering downwards, they were sweeping their fingers over the layer of gravel that coated the wire mesh base. At length, finding nothing of value, they straightened up, tipped the gravel into the pool and stood waiting for another pan-load to be brought from the pit.

A few yards away, in the shade of a small red cliff, sat the pastor. He was perched on what appeared to be a film director's chair, singing in a high voice while he watched the youths at work. The chair was dwarfed by his massive, top-heavy frame. His legs, planted on the ground before him, were thin and reedy, but his upper body was the size of an oil drum, broadening suddenly above his waist and retaining its bulk until it was reined in by his tightly-fastened white dog-collar. Out of the collar, like a giant pineapple, sprouted his crewcut-topped head, whose immensity made the spindliness of his legs seem even more miraculous.

'Aha!' he bellowed. 'A visitor from the imperial overlord!' His singing voice had been quiet, but his speaking voice boomed. 'This is wonderful! Wonderful! To what do we owe such an honour?' He sat erect, regal, his hands clasped before the barrel of his stomach. His English was precise, suggestive of a colonial-era education when a handful of privileged Africans had been well-schooled (these days, education systems on the continent were nothing more than gigantic scams to bleed foreign donors of money). His little white eyes, demonic against the dark skin of his face, creased at the edges in amusement. He had shifted his gaze from the three diamond washers for only a moment, to size me up. As he turned back to them his smirk faded. He stared intently at the young men, fearful that they would try to steal any gems they might unearth.

I introduced myself as a former employee of Feed Africa Today, the big NGO. 'An estimable organisation,' he boomed, nodding his heavy head thoughtfully. 'Wonderful. And now, Mr Hodge, you wish to move into the world of business.'

'Well -' but no sooner did I open my mouth than he interrupted me. 'It is normal,' he said, the sides of his eyes crinkling again in mirth. 'Charity work does not pay as well as business. All you whites realise this in time, and it is then that we see the limits of your altruism.' I couldn't argue with this – multinational firms operating in Africa were stuffed with former aid workers who had succumbed to the lure of private sector wages. Most of them worked in so-called Corporate Social Responsibility departments, facades erected by public relations teams to cloak their companies' pillaging in respectability and fend off the scrutiny of journalists and human rights lawyers.

'I, as you see, am a pastor,' he went on, waving his hand before his short black cape. His fingers were weighed down by gold rings, and a thicket of gold chains hung below his dog-collar. 'My name is Hubert. These boys are my flock. I am helping to rehabilitate them by giving them this work.'

I asked him where his church was. 'It is not yet in operation,' he replied, 'but I have an agreement to open a franchise here. You know Champions' Chapel, of course.' Champions' Chapel was a Nigerian megachurch founded by a carpenter. The carpenter had had a vision, in which an angel had told him that other churches' exaltation of poverty was based on a misreading of the Bible, and that Christians shouldn't be ashamed of wanting to be prosperous. In a continent mired in penury but thirsty for God's help in climbing out of it, the message had struck a chord, and the carpenter's church had spread over Africa like a vast pyramid scheme, making him and those who had joined him as pastors rich.

'Our founder is the wealthiest churchman in the world,' Hubert said proudly, his earth-shaking voice rendered less fearsome by a slight lisp. 'And he deserves every penny. Our church is transforming lives. Look at these boys.' The washers were sifting a new load of gravel on their trays. 'They were hopeless. They had fought a terrible war for nothing. They had no future. Most churches tell them that they should accept their fate and wait for the next world, but we tell them that poverty is not their portion, and that if they have belief, everything is possible.' He nodded again, smiling. 'We change their attitude from negative to positive. We are, you might say, spiritual entrepreneurs.'

He reached into his pocket and pulled out a small fold of paper. 'I believe that this is what you are looking for,' he said. He opened the paper to reveal a diamond the size of a pea. As he handed it to me I noticed that although his prim mouth was still smiling, his gaze, which had moved away from the washers to look me in the eye, had grown more intense. Still standing, since he had not offered me a seat, I held the stone before my face. It was flawless;

although uncut, it already looked like a jewel as its facets glittered in the late-afternoon light.

While I admired the cynicism behind the branding swindle that was the diamond trade, I hadn't planned to buy one of its products for the girl. But the warlord's son had put the idea into my head, and I had decided that as well as being easier to carry around than the wads of cash I'd stashed about my person, a suitably dazzling rock might be a useful back-up if she hiked her price on seeing a white man.

Money, moreover, was not a problem. I had more of it than I knew what to do with. I had been relieved of my parcel-hurling duties after one of the sultry socialists reported me for snacking on energy bars that were meant for drought victims. My defence - that the stress of the work was depleting my strength and, consequently, my productivity - was accepted only because my boss, Geoff, had once endured a similar scandal himself. Toiling in some dismal famine zone, he had been caught stuffing food parcels with dirt, whose nutritional benefits he had read about in a Latin American novel. He planned to divert the money saved to what the NGO called administrative costs (but which in fact meant expat perks like team away days at beach resorts or Christmas parties in five-star hotels). Geoff, a moody Londoner who was fond of staring at the ground and moralising, had survived because *his* boss luxuriated in showing empathy to the weak and believed everybody deserved a second chance. He gave me a cursory lecture about my behaviour, but was in no position to punish me.

Instead, to the chagrin of the sultry socialist, I was withdrawn from the frontlines and moved upstairs, promoted. I lacked the organisational skills to manage food delivery programmes, but it turned out I had a gift for fundraising. This was a stroke of luck, for not only is the role of fundraiser critical to any NGO's survival; it's also a position that involves long months when you're not expected to do anything, and therefore a perfect sinecure for those who like to keep time free for extra-curricular activity. As a fundraiser, as long as you bring in the money your work is done. How that money is spent is not your concern – your colleagues are indebted to you for keeping them on the gravy train for a few more years, and are happy for you to kick back and relax while they squander it.

A cynical mind turned out to be a useful asset in my new role. It didn't take me long to work out that successful fundraising was not a question of pitching the projects considered to be of most benefit to Africans, nor the projects Africans themselves wanted (most likely they would simply ask for cash, and the distribution of cash didn't require flights of laptops, fleets of Land Cruisers and phalanxes of aid workers). No, the key to successful fundraising was to pitch projects that would make the donor – the dispenser of funds – look good. Often donors were private companies. In our case this meant food manufacturers, whose Corporate Social Responsibility departments had decided that sponsoring a nutrition programme for underfed children would help deflect attention from their efforts to market fizzy drinks in African schools or persuade mothers who should be breastfeeding to buy powdered milk. Most of the people I was dealing with in these firms had moved into business from the aid world, thereby demonstrating their own cynicism. I was attuned to their needs, and less judgmental than my more earnest colleagues might have been.

But it wasn't only businesses that used aid projects to burnish their reputations. Traditional donors – the big international funding organisations, rich-country governments and philanthropic foundations – were also concerned primarily with looking good. When approaching them with an idea I would expound not on its usefulness, but on the publicity opportunities it would generate. Donors weren't interested in worthy but dull initiatives like handwashing promotion or seed distribution campaigns, so I sold them more photogenic projects instead. Well digging was one popular scheme (you never see a well in Africa without a plaque beside it). Food handouts were another, accompanied by colour shots of refugees receiving gruel from sacks labelled 'A Gift from the American People' or whatever. Better still, for those with deep pockets, were nutrition centres, which allowed visiting politicians to pose beside whole new buildings erected with their department's money.

Most popular of all were celebrity photo opportunities. If you can rope in somebody famous to support your project (even if that support extends no further than a ten-minute tour of the site), your hero status is assured. Politicians, diplomats and civil servants will drop everything to be snapped with a celebrity. Your colleagues, too, will be eternally grateful for the chance to have their picture taken with the bored starlet. The refugees themselves are bemused by all the fawning. 'Is this your boss?' they ask as the photographers run around shooting from all angles. 'Maybe your president?' Telling them that the yawning blonde teenager once ate cockroaches to win a cash prize on a reality show does little to clear up their confusion.

I did well, then, in my new role. I could string a sentence together to make proposals sound attractive, I had no high horse to sit on, and I had a similar perspective on the world to the government and corporate types I was selling to. And I needed to do well. Working as a fundraiser meant being transferred to Feed Africa Today's national headquarters in the capital. The women here were urban sophisticates. Although less diligent than their upcountry sisters in supporting their families, their expectations were much stiffer. These women didn't just want cash and gifts – they wanted you to take them out for dinner, lend them your credit card, accompany them on shopping sprees or take them on holiday. And the gifts they wanted were a grade up from those you had to dole out in the field. They wanted tablets, not phones; designer clothes, not fakes; foreign food, not beans and rice. I needed the higher salary to cover the expenses, and it was only after a couple of years in the new job that I attained some financial breathing space. By then the bonuses had started rolling in, and when I had to stand down, Geoff awarded me a generous severance package. After adding to this what I'd earned from the nutrition project on the island, I found myself flush with cash.

6

When Hubert proffered the diamond, therefore, I was in a good position to negotiate.

'Is this the best you have?' I asked him.

'We are just starting,' he replied, still sitting in his director's chair. 'And that is a beautiful stone. A wonderful stone.'

'But it's not certified,' I said. 'How can I get it cut and sell it if it's not certified?'

'Ah, certification,' he said. 'I see you are a man who likes to do things by the book. The only book I am governed by is the Bible.'

'Doesn't the Bible tell you to pay your taxes and respect the government?'

'There were no governments like ours when the Bible was written,' he boomed, bristling. 'When the Christians came to power I paid my taxes in full. I believed they would pave the way for our Saviour's return. But they are nothing but criminals. You appear to have been in Africa for some time, Mr Hodge - you know that if I took this diamond to them they would steal it to buy more weapons. Now I pay my taxes only to God.'

I was no more enthusiastic than he was to involve officialdom in our dealings, so we negotiated a price for the uncut stone. This, I knew, would mean that if I were to sell it instead of giving it to the girl I would have to turn to the black market, but the big diamond companies could arrange for a good stone to be certified regardless of its provenance, and despite the new regulations the trade in illegal gems remained robust.

The light was beginning to fade, although my shirt and the lining of my straw hat were as usual drenched in sweat. Overhead flew squadrons of egrets, brilliant white in the late-afternoon sun. From the pit could still be heard the arrhythmic chink of metal on rock. A steady stream of porters came over from it to the pool, bearing on their heads wok-like pans of gravel for the washers' trays. The washers, expressionless except when joking with each other about ripping the pastor off, gripped the frames tightly underwater, tipping them from side to side as they lifted them above the surface. The pastor, who looked relieved at having made a sale, kept his eyes fixed on the trays lest a stone be slipped between toes or wedged in a curl of hair.

'Why do you want a diamond anyway?' he asked me, without looking up.

'It's insurance,' I replied, not yet sure whether he was a good person to ask about the girl.

He nodded, as if I'd agreed with something he'd said. 'Wonderful!' he said. 'You think about the future.' He turned one of his gold chains like a rosary between his fingers. 'That's why you white people are rich – you put away money for a rainy day. We Africans do not do this.' His voice ratcheted up a notch in volume. 'But the future will come!' he thundered. 'You will be ready for it and we will not.'

His dog-collar was grimy with sweat. I was tired from standing for so long in the heat, regretting the excessive burden my paunch placed on my knees. I pulled out a handkerchief, careful not to disturb the diamond I'd deposited in the pocket of my shorts, and wiped my brow. Hubert continued to muse.

'It is because you think about the future that you do not cheat,' he said. 'Look at these boys,' he gestured at the washers. 'Soon we will begin to unearth more diamonds. If they stay with me they will be well rewarded. And not only in financial terms - they will be rewarded in Heaven for helping to raise up our church. But they do not think about this. All they think about is the here and now. They would steal from me in a second if I turned my back, and hightail it to the capital to sell their ill-gotten gains. There they would dissipate the money on alcohol and women before coming back to beg my forgiveness. I am a Christian, I forgive. But I have a church to establish, so for the benefit of the rest of my flock there must be limits to my tolerance.' He shook his head heavily. 'If only they thought about the future, they would be more honest. As you whites appreciate, honesty is the best policy.'

The belief that white people are more trustworthy than black was one African mystery that even after many years on the continent I struggled to understand. Despite the calamities to which upstanding white men had subjected their ancestors, Africans had often warned me that I shouldn't expect to encounter here the standards of integrity I was used to in England. The colour of my face was invariably enough to earn their confidence, even before I could open my mouth to disabuse them.

The pastor was looking pensive, threading the gold chain more quickly through his fingers. The flow of pans from the pit was slowing as the shadows lengthened, and the washers worked with less vigour as the end of another fruitless workday drew near.

'You say you left your job for more money,' Hubert continued. I had said nothing of the sort, but was not at pains to divulge the true reason for my departure. 'If you want to become a businessman, I might be able to help.'

'I don't –'.

Again he interrupted me: 'Digging this mine is only the beginning of my plans to raise up my flock,' he said. 'Of course there is the church we are building, but Champions' Chapel must spread its message not just in Africa, but far and wide. To do this I

49

have devised an ingenious scheme, to ensure the success of which I need the assistance of someone like you.'

I told him that having worked in the non-profit sector for so long I probably lacked the business experience he was seeking.

'It is not experience I need, Mr Hodge, it is people. You whites have connections – that is another example of your planning for the future. Your connections are what this project needs.'

Ignoring my attempts to dampen his enthusiasm, he explained his idea. It involved smuggling diamonds to Europe in the recta of his flock. My connections would take delivery of the rocks and have them cut, polished and sold in London. In return for agreeing to trek across the Sahara and brave the Mediterranean crossing, Hubert's messengers would each be allowed to keep a single diamond, the selling of which would enable them first to pay off the trafficker who had arranged their crossing, then to establish a foothold in Britain. Profits from the remaining diamonds – after my connections and I had taken our cut - would be wired back to help Hubert build his church.

'It is a wonderful project, with multiple benefits,' he announced, straightening in his seat and smiling as broadly as his little mouth would allow. 'Firstly, it will enable us to keep our diamonds out of the clutches of the brigands who run the government. Secondly, it will give our followers capital for when they arrive in the land of the imperial overlord – as you know, it is hard for our African brothers to make a life in a place where they are so unwelcome. And thirdly - most importantly - it will be the perfect vehicle for spreading the Word. Jesus, as I am sure you know' - a mocking glint lit his eyes - 'told us to go out into the world and preach to every creature. And where better to start than godless Europe? My boys will begin to spread the Gospel as soon as they arrive. Once the project is under way I will follow them, and I will set up a new branch of Champions' Chapel in London.'

The idea did not seem ridiculous. Europe's border police were too busy searching for drugs and Muslims to worry about diamonds, and it seemed a worthwhile project both for the smugglers and for us ("doing good to do well", as the Corporate Social Responsibility types were fond of saying). I knew someone, moreover - a former NGO colleague - who would be perfect for the job. My eyes must have betrayed hesitation, for the pastor pounced:

'So when do we start? As you see we are already unearthing diamonds, and this is just the beginning - the site is brimming with them.' He bowed his heavy head to emphasise his confidence.

I had been wary of telling a man of religion about my search for the girl, but now I had no choice. I needn't have worried. 'Ah, *that* girl,' he grinned, his watchful eyes twinkling in his dark face. 'Wonderful. You are not alone. My boys, too, were eager to possess her. Some of them almost lost their minds over her before I reined them back to sanity. They believed she would heal all their ills, but I showed them that it is only Jesus that can heal. After she had gone they thanked me for rescuing them from her spell.'

I had missed her again. It occurred to me that if I continued to move at such a leisurely pace I risked losing all trace of her. It wouldn't take long for her to put herself out of reach even of rumour, and I resolved to speed up my pursuit.

'I too saw her,' Hubert said, turning towards me and widening his eyes as if this admission should shock me. 'I believe in confronting Satan in his lair - I am not one of those pastors who shies away from the evil places of this world, using spies instead to inform me who is sinning. Nor do I seek to punish those who fall into his clutches - punishment is not for mere humans to administer. No, I seek to show them the error of their ways, to turn them from darkness to light. I, too, therefore, visit bars, and sometimes even brothels.'

A look of pride warmed his huge face. His little eyes glanced up at me, seeking my approval of his challenge to pastoral orthodoxy.

51

Finding none – chaste churchmen being as rare here as expensive prostitutes – he turned back to the washers, who had finished their work and were rolling down the soaked legs of their jeans to show him there was nothing hidden there.

He changed the subject. 'I cannot deny she was beautiful,' he said, his voice for the first time quiet. 'She seemed to be a gift from God. Her body was so supple it appeared to flow. Wonderful! It flowed like the Blue Nile through one of its gorges.' He paused. 'Before it silted up, I mean – before they dammed it. Before,' he chuckled at his wit, 'it was condemned to eternal damnation.'

'But God was testing us,' he continued, rising slowly to his feet. 'Nobody could afford her fee. Fifty thousand!' He shook his head while I took in the news of the price rise. 'Even I could not have afforded it, at least while the mine is still in its infancy. Not that I was interested, of course.' His gold chains jingled as he stretched to his full, lofty height. He took a deep breath before continuing, his voice regaining its former volume: 'Yes, the Lord was testing us. Testing our power to resist temptation. Not all, of course, stood firm. My boys were lucky they had me to watch over them. Others before them had been unable to resist. But I am surprised to discover that a representative of the imperial overlord is as easily distracted as our uneducated African boys.'

'Before them?' I said, ignoring his jibe. 'You talked to her?'

'Of course I talked to her,' he smiled indulgently as his white eyes looked down at me. 'I am a pastor. People confide in me and I hear their confessions.'

'What did she tell you?' Despite the heat, the prospect of hearing fresh news of her sent what seemed to be a shiver down my arms.

'As you know, I cannot reveal everything,' he said, enjoying his new-found power over me. 'That would be a betrayal of her confidence. All I can say is that before she came here she passed through difficult times. She is a beautiful woman – those deep eyes of hers, the tears that never fall. Of course men were tempted. I told you some of my boys went mad, and these are God-fearing boys.' He was no longer watching the washers' every move. 'Others have fewer scruples.'

'Do you mean she was attacked?' I asked, surprised how vehemently I hoped he would say no.

'She did not go into detail,' he replied, 'but I gathered that some men might have overstepped the mark.'

'When did she leave?' I asked. 'Where did she go?'

'She left a few weeks ago.' (If I hadn't lingered for so long in Itongo, I realised as a thud of frustration jolted my stomach, I would have seen her). 'I remember it because it was the day after we found our first diamond.'

'And where was she going? Did she say?'

'Not to me, but perhaps she told one of the other women.'

'Where can I find the other women?' I asked, aware that I was no longer sounding so detached.

His impish smile returned. 'Don't worry. I see that for now you are set on your deviant course. I will take you to them. Our work here is finished for the day. Now, Mr Hodge, we can relax.'

7

At a signal from their pastor, the miners began to trudge away from the pit and down the dirt path towards the cars. Rousing my driver, who had fallen asleep at the foot of the red cliff, we followed. After a few hundred yards, at a junction I had not noticed on our way in, the path divided into three. Most of the miners turned left. We and the remaining men took the rightward track, arriving half an hour later, after climbing a small rise, at a long, single-storey building in whose corrugated-iron façade were reflected the last, glinting rays of the setting sun.

'This,' Hubert told me, 'is for the workers who come from far away. Those others come from a village in the forest. They go home at night to their wives. But these boys do not have homes to go to. Their villages did not survive the war - some of them destroyed them with their own hands. So we built this hostel for them. And here,' he beckoned me to follow him around the building, 'is the relaxation area.'

In the shade to the rear of the hostel stood a large, gazebo-like structure with a thatched roof. Plastic tables were dotted around the hard-packed earth floor. Welcoming us inside, the pastor directed us to a table occupied by three beautiful women in tight, low-cut vests. As we took our seats, one of them rose to pass us bottles of warm Warthog from a stack of beer crates.

'It's not a church then?' I said to Hubert, who had loosened his dog-collar and was sitting between me and the most sumptuous of the women.

He smiled. 'As I told you, our church has not yet been built. My boys and I pray together at the mine each morning before we start to dig. This is where they rest after a hard day doing God's work.'

'And you allow women in here?'

'Of course!' he boomed, laughing at my naivety. 'How else am I to show them the light? How else can they receive God's mercy? After I counsel them, they are persuaded of the error of their ways. They decide to change their lives, and to seek out other professions or find husbands and start families. It is wonderful to see the transformation. Wonderful!'

'What about the girl?' I said. 'Did you transform her?'

He looked down at the ground. 'I tried to help her too,' he said, resignation dulling the glow of his eyes. 'But her mind was made up. Her ears were closed to Christ's message. There was nothing I could do.'

Like so many beautiful young women, he told me, the girl had fallen into prostitution because there was no alternative. She had left her home village suddenly, for reasons she didn't reveal to Hubert, and set up as a market trader in a nearby town. The venture was not a success. 'She did not have a business brain,' Hubert smiled ruefully. 'She gave credit to the wrong people. Both her suppliers and her customers took advantage of her.'

'She probably charged too much,' the woman sitting next to Hubert butted in, tapping the ash from a half-smoked cigarette into a tin ashtray. 'She thought she was too good.'

The woman beside her, who had been staring at her reflection in the screen of her phone, looked up and shook her head. 'She never seemed arrogant to me,' she said. 'She was kind and gentle. I don't know why she kept her price so high, but I don't think it was because she thought she was better than us.'

'Maybe poor men don't satisfy her in bed,' the first woman sneered, 'so she priced herself out of their reach.' Around her head was tied a dark blue scarf. On a silver chain between her lavish breasts hung a tiny square frame containing a swirl of black and blue and white. I wondered whether it might be one of those Middle Eastern charms that ward off the evil eye, but my thoughts soon strayed to the pendant's buxom backdrop.

'You were jealous because she was more beautiful than us,' said the third woman, the youngest, whose plaited blond hair extensions reached almost to the ground.

'I wasn't jealous.' The woman sucked slowly on her cigarette, the tell-tale appurtenance of a full-time pro in a continent where, despite aggressive marketing campaigns by Western tobacco companies, few women smoked. I realised as she spoke that she was looking not at her colleagues but at me. 'It's not all about beauty,' she said. 'Yes, she was beautiful. The brown of her eyes was as deep as the beat of a chief's drum when he called his people to deliver news of a death.' The other women and the pastor nodded, their faces turned floorwards, remembering. 'In the days when people listened to the chiefs, I mean,' she continued. 'Before they prostituted themselves to the white man.'

The miners were sitting in groups at the other tables, drinking beer or cassava gin. Some had been joined by girls who had materialised from the bush. Night had fallen, bringing with it the usual mosquito air raid. Someone had switched on the radio – through its crackly speaker came the sound of country music, whose undemanding tones were strangely popular in this part of Africa.

The woman with the pendant was still looking at me. Her scarf, wrapped tightly around her head, seemed to be pulling the edges of her dark eyes back and upwards from her fine, high cheekbones. With her unblemished skin and fulsome curves I found it hard to imagine anyone could outstrip her in beauty. She had lit another cigarette off her last one. She inhaled deeply. 'But it's not just about how you look,' she went on, allowing the smoke to filter slowly from her lips. 'You have to work hard too. She expected to make a living without working hard. When nobody could afford her she relied on bar owners to look after her. I want to fend for myself, not depend on others.'

'But she never asked for anything,' the second woman said. 'The bar owners helped her because she brought in customers.'

'Valerie here has no tolerance for idlers,' Hubert broke in, a knowing smile indenting his dark cheeks. 'She has an excellent business brain. She is not like the one we are discussing - none of her clients pulls a fast one on her.'

Valerie looked at me defiantly. You will have me tonight, her eyes seemed to be saying, but you will pay me well for the privilege. I hauled my eyes away, determined not to become embroiled.

Hubert took a slug of beer and leaned his heavy head closer to mine. 'I would like to involve her in our little venture,' he said. 'People like Valerie are difficult to find around here. She would be an excellent recruit to Champions' Chapel, but she is proving a tough nut to crack. It sometimes seems that the harder I strive to draw her away from her sinful beliefs, the farther away she drifts. Recently she has been threatening to leave us and make her way to the westernmost extremities of Africa. That, as you know, is thousands of miles away, as far away from here as she could possibly go.' He looked at her and sighed. 'The Lord, as you see,' he said, turning back to me, 'likes to test his servants.'

Impressed by her shunning of the pastor's advances, and perceiving an opportunity to soften her hard veneer by showing an interest in her life and not just her cleavage, I asked Valerie about her travel plans. Her father, she told me, had come from west to central Africa to mine gold and diamonds and to spread the word of Islam. He was a member of a mystical brotherhood which encouraged hard work and prayer as a means of drawing closer to God. He had gained many converts to his cause, and also acquired a considerable fortune. 'He owned dozens of mines and hundreds of cows,' Valerie said proudly, ignoring the incessant shaking of Hubert's lumbering head. 'Our compound had seven houses.' In the war, Christian soldiers had taken over her father's mines and looted his home. As he fled with his family into the bush, he looked back at the seven pillars of smoke rising from the ruins.

The central African bush was no place for an aging couple, and he and his wife were soon carried off by disease. Their children scattered, destitute, but a group of the man's converts had clubbed together to send his and his wife's bodies to be buried in the land of their ancestors. Their daughter, her life saved by prostitution, was hoping to put by enough money to visit their graves. 'The city where they were laid to rest is the sacred home of our dear sheikh,' she said, stubbing out a cigarette without lighting a new one. 'Our sheikh was a great man - he defied the white Christians and stood by his religion. They couldn't lead him astray.' She shot a glance at the pastor, who in order to shield their ears from such heresies had loudly engaged the other two women in conversation.

'Look at this,' she said. She beckoned me closer, and as I stood and leaned across the table she thrust her gleaming breasts up towards my eyes. Slowly but inexorably I felt my resolve to resist her crumbling. Behind me I could sense Hubert's horrified glare as my face advanced to within tongue's length of her glistening, almond-coloured cleavage. The other tables, too, had fallen silent, leaving the bar's crackly airwaves to a country singer who was crooning about her cheating lover.

Just when it seemed I could lean no closer without burrowing between her breasts in humiliating abandonment, Valerie lifted a finger towards my chin. I thought for a thrilling moment that she was about to guide me in, like a honeyguide bird directing the hunter to the most succulent honeycomb in the forest, but instead she slid her fingertip under the pendant and raised it before my crestfallen eyes. 'This is our sheikh,' she said. I had to lift my head away slightly to see what she was talking about, but now that I was forced to look properly I could see that the pendant depicted not just a wash of colours but the figure of a dark-skinned man in a white robe. The man was kneeling on a mat laid out on the rippling waves of a deep blue sea. To one side of him towered an enormous black steamer under a French flag. In the surrounding sea, fish poked their heads above the surface to find out what was happening.

'Here he is,' Valerie explained, 'returning from exile. The French thought they could stop us by taking away our leader, but it only made us stronger. They had to release him because they were afraid we would rise up against them. Look at the size of their ship! They wouldn't let him pray on board, so he made it wait while he knelt on the waves of the ocean. When I reach his city I will worship at the Great Mosque where he is buried. The money you pay me will help me fulfil my obligations to the community when I arrive.'

I sat down, deflated. Hubert was rolling his eyes. 'These are the tests the Lord sends us,' he sighed. 'For every one we convert there are many more who remain lost.'

The bar was emptying as the miners drifted off with their women. I asked Valerie if she knew where the girl had gone.

'Probably to New York or Paris,' she scoffed. 'Africa's not good enough for her.'

'She went to Tishioni on the coast,' the blonde girl said quietly.

'Tishioni?' I said, surprised. 'Why would she go there?' Tishioni, as far as I knew, was not only nearly a thousand miles northeast of here but was also a staunchly Muslim town where Sharia law was administered by a strict religious police force. Even for the most beautiful prostitute in Africa, it seemed unlikely to be fertile territory.

Hubert motioned to the blonde girl to bring us another beer. 'Tishioni is not all it seems,' he said. 'First of all, since it is a coastal town there is a Christian community there, descendants of the earliest converts. So there are bars where alcohol is served - in moderation of course - and where you might find a few working girls. The community is small but it is strong, standing its ground in the midst of the heathen hordes.' Valerie returned his smirk with a glare. 'And second,' he continued, 'the so-called Muslim religious police are not quite, shall we say, as pure as they expect others to be.'

'Sounds a bit like some pastors,' Valerie retorted. 'Has he told you about the money he takes from the girls as penance when they confess? Or what he gets from the ones who don't have any money?' Hubert shook his head and laughed, but failed to hide his uneasiness as he fingered his dog-collar. Valerie turned to the other women and continued her tirade: 'You know those white men who want to save you as well as fuck you?' Her colleagues laughed nervously. 'Some of our black pastors are like that too.'

Hubert looked to me for support. 'As I told you, Mr Hodge,' he said, 'sometimes we fail. Satan is a powerful enemy. If you are determined to pursue your errant course, you must be careful. Tishioni is full of hypocrites. There are policemen who would extort money from their own grandmothers. They have networks of spies who inform them about adulterers and fornicators. They are barbarians, heathens. They will certainly burn in hell.'

I didn't think that as a foreigner and a nominal Christian I would be an obvious target for Tishioni's religious police force, and was in any case no longer in the market for fornication. Although I was unsure whether the slim prospect of finding the girl there merited a thousand-mile journey in a packed bush taxi, I had no other leads. The next morning, after a torrid night with Valerie (whose advances I proved powerless to repel), my driver took me back to Itongo to catch transport to the east.

8

It was still dark when I arrived at the bus stand, a patch of dry earth ringed by abandoned tin shacks. There were no buses - only three battered estate cars rusting quietly in one corner. These vehicles have no fixed schedule, but leave when they are full. And I mean full. Unless each row of seats cushions twice as many backsides as it was designed for, the driver won't deign to take his place at the helm. Only when every square foot of room is occupied by at least two contorted bodies might he think about turning the key in the ignition. Even this, however, is less a signal of imminent departure than a ruse to persuade wavering would-be passengers that the vehicle is ready to leave. Passengers arriving at transport parks head for the most crowded vehicles, those that appear least comfortable, for only these have any chance of setting off that day. A vehicle that is still half-empty an hour after dawn will remain half-empty until the earth has pirouetted on its axis. You might as well go back to bed.

When I saw the three empty cars I was tempted not only to go back to Valerie's love nest (since she charged by the minute to attract impoverished miners, she had been happy to humour my laboured efforts), but to put on hold my search for the girl. I could see no more than half a dozen other potential travellers, and most of these were probably decoys paid by a driver to make it look like his conveyance contained passengers. It would be hours, possibly days, before we departed, and the prospect of sitting bent double for two or three days in one of these cramped, clapped-out vehicles filled me with gloom.

And for what, I asked myself. I wasn't even sure the girl existed, much less that I would find her at the end of the ride. There were beautiful women all over Africa – how could I be confident everybody had been talking about the same one? I began to wonder whether my sacking might have affected my mental stability, the curtailment of my happy depravity somehow knocking me off balance. My thoughts were taking unfamiliar turns. The attempt to find the girl seemed to give me purpose, but my life had never had any purpose beyond self-gratification and this hadn't mattered before. And the sacking hadn't really bothered me. I was a little needled that one of the sultry socialists had finally got one over on me (for she it was who stumbled across my indiscretion in the woods outside the refugee camp and gleefully reported it to my superiors), but she was probably doing me a favour – as the women had grown more demanding, and as my aging libido slumped in parallel with their efforts to arouse it, charity work had lost much of its lustre.

Nor would it be difficult, once the fuss had died down, to get back into the industry. Aid workers pride themselves on their ability to empathise with human weakness; nothing (except the misdeeds of Western governments and businesses) is anyone's fault. Even the most bloodthirsty of African dictators is a product of history, or of childhood trauma, or of the greed of Western governments and businesses. Somebody who merely flouts his organisation's code of conduct is therefore easy to forgive. Not everyone, they know, is strong enough to withstand the pressures of being a humanitarian; a few will inevitably buckle under the strain. All I needed was a little time to rest, reflect and acknowledge the error of my ways. Then I could be welcomed back with nods of self-satisfied understanding into the fold. Besides, the deal I'd made with Geoff to take the flak for the whole episode guaranteed me a glowing reference should I ever choose to return.

You might, if you haven't already guessed, be wondering what I did to be relieved of my duties, although what I did is slightly different from what I was reported to have done. What I was reported to have done was to break the NGO's Rule Number 1: Do Not Screw The Clients (I paraphrase from the code-of-conduct jargon). What I did was more innocent, but the sultry socialist took a picture of me in a compromising position with the rather beautiful internally displaced person (or IDP as they are known in the trade), photoshopped it for dramatic effect on her designer smartphone, and marched into Geoff's office demanding my head.

Geoff, worried that she might send the picture to the British press if he ignored her, had no choice but to accede to her wishes (the right-wing tabloids had whole teams working on stories that discredited the aid industry). When rumours spread about the donor's involvement in the incident, he had no choice but to accede quickly. For I was not alone in my imprudence. I had taken the representative of one of our biggest funders out into the field to show him how hungry everybody was (these field trips and the generous *per diems* that came with them were a good way of supplementing one's salary). As was my habit, I had also treated him to a little corporate hospitality. After a few lunchtime Warthogs and cassava gins in the refugee camp's louchest bar, the donor, a jovial Scandinavian, went off with one its more exotic working girls – a pygmy – leaving me alone with the beautiful IDP.

It should be noted, in my defence, that I hadn't known the woman was a refugee. Until she informed me that her good looks had secured her the role of showing visitors around the camp, I had taken her for a local NGO official. By this time, however, she was kneeling between my legs on the leaf-strewn ground and whispering over my exhilarated member. Although the chastest missionary would have struggled to call a halt at that point – as

Geoff sympathetically acknowledged – none of this would save me. Her being internally displaced, a refugee in her own country, was beyond the pale, and gave the sultry socialist the opportunity she'd been waiting for. The donor reluctantly let me take the blame – the scandal, he said, might have not only brought down his government but caused permanent embarrassment to a country that prided itself on its compassion for the less fortunate.

My musings were interrupted by the honk of a horn. One of the cars had filled up surprisingly quickly, and its driver was urging me to take the last remaining space. Realising that I had nothing better to do, and that a prompt departure would give us a chance of arriving in Tishioni the following day, I decided to get in.

I squeezed into the seat behind the driver. There were five people on this seat, which had been designed by its defunct European manufacturer for three. My head was jammed up against the roof, which sagged under the weight of the luggage tied on top. Hemming in my feet was an assortment of jerry cans, machetes, holdalls and live chickens. A faint smell of sweat and manure permeated the cabin: nuzzling the legs of the passengers in the row behind us were two full-size goats.

The driver, a teenage boy with a baseball cap and a plastic silver crucifix, gunned the engine. It sputtered grudgingly into life and, with the help of a push from two decoy passengers, moved off across the bumpy dirt. As we pulled out onto the road, a man in a white pharmacist's coat and light blue skullcap ran out in front of the car and slammed his hands on the bonnet. The driver stopped, and the man, whose girth was wide enough for two people, pulled open the door beside me and bundled in. We moved off again, trundling through the hacked-down forest and the abandoned, disintegrating villages.

To accommodate the new arrival's bulk, and since he quickly made himself comfortable spreading out across the seat back, the other passengers in the row had to lean forward. 'Hey, keep that manky leg away from me,' the man said after a while, looking down at a large sore that had developed on the inside of my left thigh after one of my romps with the girl in Itongo. I squeezed my legs closer together. 'What are you doing here anyway?' he said in the local language. Leaning forward with my chest almost touching my raised knees, I stared ahead, hoping he would give up if I pretended not to understand him. From the corner of my eye I could see his red, henna-dyed beard working as he spoke. 'Have you come to steal our diamonds like all the rest of the bastards?' he persisted. I half-turned to him. His mouth was cavernous, like the door of a baker's furnace. On the top of his nose was a bulbous, hairy wart.

I told him I worked for an NGO.

'Same thing,' he retorted. 'All that's just a front for your looting. You give us an inch and take a mile. And you expect us to be grateful. Hah!' He snorted, then spat explosively out of the window. 'If I had my way we'd kick out the lot of you. You whites are nothing but leeches. You're a cancer on our continent.'

I shifted in my seat, unused to such vitriol in a part of Africa characterised by its languor. Most of the other passengers had fallen asleep, their heads on their knees or on neighbours' shoulders. Two teenage boys further along our row were grinning at the man's chutzpah. The few older passengers who were still awake were looking out through the windows, keeping their thoughts to themselves.

'What takes you to Tishioni?'' I asked him, trying to change the subject.

'That's where I live,' he said. 'I've been on holiday.'

'Holiday?' I said, surprised.

'Yeah, I've been in what you Europeans call the heart of Africa. Now I'm going home.'

'You must have a bit of money to make that journey,' I said (the concept of a holiday would have been alien to most Africans I knew).

'I have plenty of money,' he said, his wide nostrils flaring with pride. 'I'm a miller. Thanks to you whites, my business is booming.'

'Oh, we do some good then,' I said.

'Yeah, you whites destroyed the climate so there's no grass left for cattle herders. These days they have to buy their feed, and I mill it for them.' He was referring to the few remaining nomads of the east African scrub, whose way of life – slow days roaming under the sun in search of water and pasture for their herds - was doomed.

'And that brings in enough money to take holidays abroad?' I asked.

'He probably puts dust in the grain,' one of the teenage boys smirked.

'I'd shut my mouth if I were you,' the miller said, 'unless you'd prefer me to shut it for you.' The boy, his brow pressed against the headrest of the passenger seat in front of him, mumbled something to his friend. 'There's no respect nowadays,' the man continued. 'That's another thing you whites polluted us with – now anyone can say anything, even to their elders.'

Looking out of the front window, I could see what he had meant about the herders' predicament. As we had left the stumpy forest behind us, the land had dried out. Dreary ochre plains stretched off into the distance, the only trees a few leafless baobabs. Signs of human habitation were limited to the shores of dried-out lakes or the banks of extinct rivers. Mud houses that in better days had risen out of the earth were now crumbling back into it, the settlements of which they once formed part abandoned to the hot wind that was coating the passengers of the estate car in dust. The pitted dirt road, like the land around it, was empty, and it occurred to me that in the likely event of a breakdown we risked dying of thirst while we waited for another vehicle to assist us.

The miller fell asleep and began snoring loudly. I must have dropped off too, for in the late afternoon I awoke to find that the car had stopped and that my arm was being shaken by a khaki-clad soldier. He spoke a language I didn't know (although studying French and Portuguese at university had prepared me well for post-colonial Africa, the local languages I'd learned to make life easier when buttering up women did not include his), but it was obvious he wanted me to get out of the car.

The other passengers had already alighted, and were standing around grumbling about the interruption to the journey. The miller was off to one side, kneeling on a mat in the dust and praying. I climbed out and stretched my creaking limbs. We appeared to have passed through a small village, whose mud houses retained their straw roofs and on whose eastern edge, where we had stopped, a gaggle of crouching women were hawking peanuts and cups of hot millet gruel to the checkpoint's captives.

The soldier, a lean young man in dark glasses, pointed with his pistol at my bag, which had been tied to the roof of the car. I took it down and placed it on the ground before him, and knelt to unhook the safety pins that served as a zip (the holdall was Chinese-made – its original fastener had broken off the first time I'd closed it). Following his instructions, I began to pile the bag's contents onto the chair he had brought out from his straw shelter. There was nothing that might interest him and, bored of watching, he ordered me to re-pack the bag before I'd finished emptying it. As we climbed back into the car the other passengers complained that the soldier had singled out a foreigner. They grumbled in agreement when one of the teenage boys surmised that he must have regarded me – at least until he saw the state of my bag - as the most likely source of a bribe.

In the village the driver had found a couple of bottles of petrol and a jerry can of water. He poured the petrol into the tank through a plastic funnel and opened the bonnet to top up the water. We moved off again down the dirt road, but after a few seconds heard shouting from the rear. The car stopped, and I was surprised to see a gasping, hollow-faced young white man in a tattered black jacket leaning to ask the driver if he could join us. The driver assented, and he opened the passenger door and squeezed in. The seat was occupied by two others, but the newcomer was so thin that after his neighbours had shifted to their left there was still room for the driver to manoeuvre the gear stick and resume the journey.

Our new companion looked round, acknowledging his neighbours and the miller but ignoring me. This was not unusual – there was a certain type of Western expat in Africa who, in an effort to appear integrated, would go to extreme lengths to fraternise with local people rather than with other whites. In towns popular with international NGOs - towns, that is, with plenty of amenities, fast internet connections, clement weather and an airport - you would often see such characters in the restaurants of expensive hotels, eating with their fingers while their African friends grappled with knives and forks. On occasion I had spotted sultry socialists in such circumstances, their braided hair tied back to expose the tattoos of Africa etched on their pretty necks. Most of the time these self-described Old Africa Hands would act as if other white people didn't exist. When they couldn't avoid them, they would demonstrate their old-timer credentials by slipping into the conversation the few words they knew of the local language.

This one probably took me for a tourist or a businessman, tribes he would have viewed with contempt. I greeted him loudly in English, and he grunted in reply.

'Get stranded?' I asked amiably.

'The car I was in broke down,' he said, 'and I'm in a bit of a hurry.' He felt he had to excuse his abandonment of a sinking ship, a ship whose other passengers wouldn't have had the money to jump into another vehicle. He fumbled with the top of his plastic water bottle. On his lap his holdall, open at the top, bulged with hardback books.

'You have come to save us too, I suppose,' the miller joined in brusquely.

The young man was taken aback. 'No, no, I'm a writer. I try to increase understanding of Africa, not save it.'

I was unable to suppress a snort.

'What are you writing about?' The miller's tone had grown less gruff, writers retaining an aura in Africa that they had long since lost in the West. 'And what are you doing out here in this godforsaken bush?' His English, I noticed, was more refined than his use of the local language.

'Well, the two are related.' The writer, warming to his theme, had half-turned to face us. His skin was pale, and his lank, mousy hair stuck sweatily to his temples. 'I'm writing a book about great African leaders,' he said. 'I've been travelling around the continent researching them, and talking to ordinary Africans to find out how they are remembered.'

'And where have you been? There are not many great African leaders around here,' the miller chuckled.

'Oh I'm just passing through on my way to the coast,' the writer said. 'I've been all around Africa, though I must admit my research hasn't borne much fruit yet.'

He had been travelling for months, he told us, journeying thousands of miles around the west and middle of the continent, but had been unable to enter any of the countries he had planned to visit.

'They're all too unstable at the moment,' he explained, his face oozing empathy. 'The British government advises against travelling to them.'

'All of them?' the miller asked. 'I have just been to the country that lies at the very heart of Africa and I survived.'

'Yes, I'd hoped to go there too, but they're all either at war or threatened by rebellions or terrorism. It's ridiculous, of course – we're much more likely to get killed in this car than by terrorists. The British government is overcautious, but if you go to countries on their red list your insurance is invalid, so if you fall sick or have an accident you have to pay from your own pocket to be flown home for treatment. As you can see' – he opened his arms to show us his faded jacket and his threadbare, sweat-soaked white shirt – 'I don't have the money for that.'

The miller was laughing so loudly that a few of the other passengers woke up. 'So you did not go to any of them?' he said between guffaws. 'Because of insurance? Do we Africans have insurance? Can we call up a helicopter to evacuate us if we come down with a fever?'

'Your politicians can,' I said, feeling sorry for my beleaguered compatriot.

'Yes, you whites are like our politicians. You think you are special. You think your lives are worth more than ours. You talk about helping us, but when the shit hits the fan' - as he reverted to his earthier phraseology he enunciated the consonants with spat venom – 'we see what you really think.'

The writer was facing forwards again, blushing and fumbling with his water bottle. 'Once I've done some more background research I hope to go back,' he said quietly, 'but I'm going home for a while first.' The estate car trudged across the dusty brown plains. The sun was low in the sky, and it would not be many more hours before we would have to stop in some desolate village for the night.

'And why are you writing this book anyway?' the miller asked, no longer laughing.

'Because when people in the West think about African leaders they think only about the most nefarious ones. They think about the torture and the killings, or about the corruption and the opulence. Because of this they see African people as helpless and hopeless, as victims. I want to show that there has also been a different kind of leader, one who wanted to help his country, to stand up to colonial oppression, and to make Africa stand on its own feet instead of depending on handouts from the West.'

'So you wanted to write about the Saviour of the Nation,' the miller said, stroking the hairs sprouting from his nose-wart. 'I have just been on holiday in his country. Without insurance.' He winked at me. 'I went to see his palace in the jungle. A beautiful place. It once had jade walls and gold taps. It was known as the Versailles of the jungle. Now *there* was an African leader.'

The writer frowned. 'No, that's who everyone thinks of when African leaders are discussed, and that's my point. I'm writing about that leader's predecessor, who told the world about the humiliations of colonialism and the theft of Africa's raw materials by foreign powers, and who refused to bow to the West. But as I said, I couldn't get into the country so I've had to postpone my research.'

'That bow tie-wearing communist!' The miller looked bemused. 'You think kowtowing to the Russians helped Africa stand on its own two feet? The Cold War hadn't touched us until he begged the commies for support – after that we had them and the Yanks crawling all over the continent.' He shook his big head. 'And who else, in your wisdom, do you regard as a great African leader?'

The writer, still facing forwards, reeled off a list of once-promising figures from the countries he had tried to visit. Most had either led their nations' efforts to gain independence or, when independence turned out not to bring the expected freedom from colonial interference, attempted in vain to shake off Western influence once and for all.

'Nobody in Europe or America has heard of these men,' he said, his thin voice almost a whine. 'Whenever people there write about Africa it's about the negative things, never the positive. There have been great African leaders, but they don't fit our stereotypes so they are forgotten.'

The miller leant forward towards him, squeezing the rest of us back into our seats. Speaking quietly, with a hint of menace in his voice, he said: 'Two things: First, none of your so-called great leaders survived. They are all dead. They all failed. They were naïve. Only the strong leaders were able to stand up to the West, the clever ones like the Lion Warrior, the ones who played them at their own devilish game.' The writer didn't look round.

'And second,' the miller hissed, the hairs on his wart receding as his nostrils widened: 'Who gives a FUCK about what people in the West think?' The writer jumped in his seat. 'They do not care what we think of them. Why should we care what they think of us? All they want is to exploit us – that is all they have wanted for five hundred years. And even if what they thought did matter, it is not your weak, dead leaders we should show them. It is strong leaders like the Supreme Combatant, leaders who outwit them, who are more powerful than them - leaders who endure.'

The writer pursed his thin lips and nodded tamely.

'You probably think of the All-Powerful Warrior as a thief,' the miller continued, working his way through the sobriquets his hero had given himself. 'And if you regard stealing from the Americans as theft, you would be correct. But he was merely reclaiming a small fraction of what the West has stolen from our continent over the centuries. He was a hero to his people. You know he was a writer, like you?'

The writer raised his eyebrows.

'You see? You research all these failures, but you accept the Western lies about our strong African leaders. He was a journalist before he became a soldier. He reported on the Europeans' crimes in his country. That is how your communist friend was able to drum up so much support for kicking the Europeans out. But your friend wanted to sell our country to the Russians. His successor, the

Great Leader who Moved from Conquest to Conquest Leaving Fire in his Wake, made it African again.'

This, I knew, was specious - the name the dictator had given his country in order to "Africanise" it derived from a Portuguese word, and the uniforms he had had his officials wear were copied from Maoist China. But I was too tired by now to intervene. Dusk had been and gone, and the unpopulated scrub outside was pitch dark. Mosquitoes flew in the open windows and buzzed around the heads of the sleeping passengers. One of the teenage boys switched on a small radio. A football match was being broadcast on the only station he could find, but since it was from the capital rather than from Europe he switched it off.

The writer, too, had had enough. Avoiding the miller's challenging gaze, he turned his attention to me. 'Are you the one who's looking for the girl?' he said.

'How do you know?'

'I was mistaken for you a couple of times on my way here.'

'Oh yes?' the miller smirked and elbowed me hard in the ribs. 'What girl's this?' he said, slipping back into the local tongue. 'The whore?'

'You know about her?' I said, surprised to find myself slightly flustered.

'Everybody knows about her,' he cackled. 'Even our serious writer man here knows about her, you see? You whites aren't so high-minded when you have the chance to fuck one of our African women. You stop feeling bad about exploiting us when you see a pair of glossy black legs spread before you.'

'Have you seen her?' I asked the writer.

'I saw her from afar, yes. In a town not far from Itongo.'

'Where was she going?' I felt like an explorer who had received concrete news of a place whose existence he was beginning to doubt. 'What did she look like?'

The glow of oil lamps on the ground by the road showed we had reached the outskirts of a village. Behind them, dark women crouched beside meagre piles of vegetables scattered on scraps of cloth. 'She was leaving in a car like this,' he replied. 'People said she was going east. I couldn't really see her, except in profile. But even from afar you could see she was beautiful. That liquid glint in her eye, the unsullied darkness of her skin. But the thing that stayed with me was the elegance of her neck. It was so graceful and slender, as straight as honour.' He risked a glance at the miller. 'Before the world discarded honour, I mean, as something it no longer needed.'

'Very profound,' the miller said in English, forcing us forward as he leaned back and stretched out. 'Is her pussy beautiful too, as succulent as the ripest mango on its last evening before it falls from the tree?' He chuckled to himself. 'And do her fingers move softly yet quickly, like the wings of the Madagascan moon moth before the Chinese built a football stadium over its last habitat?'

'You haven't seen her then?' I said.

'No, but I have heard about her. You know about the stabbing I suppose?' He looked triumphant when I shook my head. 'Two men fought over her with knives. They say one ended up with an extra hole in his backside.' He laughed loudly. 'It seems you have heard she is in Tishioni?'

'I've no idea where she is,' I said, eager to throw him off the scent. 'I've given up looking.'

He saw through my weak deceit. 'Oh, you needn't worry about me,' he laughed. 'As you see,' he tipped his head, showing me his cap, 'I am a Muslim. I already have four wives, and I have no interest in impure whores.'

The car pulled up by a dimly-lit single-storey building. It was unmarked, but from the doorways along the grubby corridor leading away from the street I could tell it was a guest house, probably doubling as a brothel. The passengers climbed out of the car, stretching and yawning. The miller disappeared inside. Espying a stack of beer crates at the far end of the corridor, I made to follow him, but the writer held me by the arm and stopped me. 'You heard how she got into prostitution?' he said, his pallid face given vigour by his earnestness.

'You know about that?' I said, surprised. 'I heard she'd failed in business.'

'That was later,' he said. 'The reason she became a market woman in the first place was to escape the clutches of a politician.'

'How do you know this?'

'I've done some research. She sounded interesting so I made a few enquiries. She's a secretive person, so what I heard is based on rumour, but I managed to gather a few snippets of information.'

With his hand he brushed his hair back from his face, as if preparing to deliver a lesson.

'She was the most beautiful girl in her province,' he said. 'Every man wanted to marry her. But her family was poor, the poorest in her village, and she was an asset for them. Even if her parents hadn't wanted her to, her more distant relatives would have insisted she marry someone wealthy. So they allowed only rich men to visit her. Of course all these men brought gifts to dazzle the relatives. You know, mobile phones, sunglasses, that kind of junk.' The other passengers had disappeared and we stood alone by the car. The village streets around us were deserted and dark.

'Finally,' he continued, 'the family decided on the richest man of all, a politician who came from a big, far-off city bearing smartphones and flat-screen televisions for all the relatives, and who promised to give them all jobs on public works projects. But the girl ran away before the wedding. Some say she found the politician repellent - and who wouldn't? Others say she couldn't bear the idea of being bought. Whatever it was, it's uplifting, don't you think? To hear of a poor African standing up to the system. And a woman at that.'

'Not very uplifting for her parents,' I said, more to puncture his excitement than as a judgement of the girl's actions.

'They're OK – I heard she sends them money whenever she can. The other relatives must be upset, but for them she was just a cash cow. They didn't care what happened to her as long as they got their TVs and their corruptly-acquired jobs.'

We went inside. I grabbed a few bottles of Warthog from the crates at the back and took them to the cell-like room to which the hotel's female proprietor showed me. She offered to keep me company, but I declined and she moved off towards the writer's room.

It was several hours before I fell asleep. The girl had scrambled my mind. I had been relieved that the miller wasn't interested in her, and was envious of the writer's knowledge of her past. Her behaviour, moreover – her humility and kindness, her unwillingness to reduce her price, her rejection, in spurning the politician, of easy wealth – mystified me. Some of it seemed to border on the insane. Neither her refusal to be sold nor her distaste for her wealthiest suitor tallied with her prostitution. Her uncompromisingly high fee and her rejection of the politician's gifts sounded masochistic. I could fathom neither her motives nor her movements, and this failure, in a world whose machinations I had thought, as a cynic, I understood, unsettled me.

In the morning the writer and a few of the other passengers had gone, leaving the rest of us a little more room in the car. The vehicle, however, would not start. The driver had no ideas for resolving the problem other than to pour water into the engine. Amateur mechanics appeared from the village and tinkered for hours to no avail. By the evening the miller was growing impatient. 'I have a business to run,' he announced. I had a girl to track down, but knew that losing my calm would be futile.

By the next morning the miller was furious. He marched out of the guest house and, seeing the car's passenger door open with the driver asleep across the seats, slammed it with such force that it came off its hinges and fell to the ground. The driver awoke with a start and sat up. With a mighty kick the miller next removed the front bumper, before moving round to take aim at the door on the driver's side. To escape him, but forgetting in his drowsiness the car's plight, the driver turned the key in the ignition. Nothing happened. The miller kicked his door hard. As if to avoid another pounding, the car coughed into life. Without turning the engine off, the driver got out and calmly manoeuvred the stricken passenger door back into place, securing it with a wire looped back through the open window of the rear door. We resumed our journey at last and, with the driver unwilling to risk another breakdown by stopping, arrived in Tishioni in the late afternoon.

9

Tishioni's bus stand, like many others across the continent, was a bare patch of open ground. Unlike in other bus stands, however, the young men milling about here did not spring into a frenzy the moment they spotted a white limb poking out of a newly-arrived vehicle. Normally in these places I would be mobbed by touts before my foot touched dry earth, with offers ranging from motorbike-taxi rides and hotel rooms to prostitutes and precious stones. Here, I was left alone. Even when I was fully disembarked, with my bag standing between my legs, nobody so much as shouted "hey, white man" at me.

At first I took this lack of interest to be a positive sign. I'd heard that Tishioni was a prosperous city, grown plump on exports of fish, livestock and textiles - perhaps its inhabitants had more constructive things to do than harass foreigners. It was only when I noticed that my fellow passengers had had no trouble finding rides into town that I realised it might be *because* of my skin colour that I'd been left marooned.

I looked around. On the edges of the bus stand, young men stood about in groups. Many wore the usual European cast-off T-shirts and jeans, but others were robed in long, white or pastel-coloured tunics, and nearly all sported flat-topped, brimless cloth caps embroidered with Quranic script or images of Mecca. The men were looking in my direction, but none appeared to be speaking.

As I stood in the middle of the bus stand by the empty estate car, the fierce sun conjuring sweat from all parts of my body while black plastic bags blew in a hot breeze around my ankles, I felt a loneliness that Africa had seldom allowed me. I was exposed, vulnerable, like a bull waiting for the start of the corrida. There was nothing for it but to pick up my bag and walk eastwards, towards the sea, where I hoped I might find a hotel that was used to foreigners.

I opted for the busiest street. Paved and in good condition, it was flanked by dark, cavernous stores with open doorways. Inside them were piled bulging sacks of rice or grain imported from Asia. Motorcycle-taxis sped noisily past me in both directions, carrying people, live goats, mattresses, iron bars and planks of wood. Rickshaws churned by more slowly, loaded with passengers. There were larger vehicles too, trucks and jeeps - the first, other than Hubert's Hummer, that I had seen for weeks. Alleys off to one side led to a market, where women, their heads and shoulders draped in brightly-coloured scarves, haggled over mounds of fruit and vegetables that looked a good deal fresher and more copious than those that had been on offer in Itongo and on the island. It struck me again that there was wealth here, which made it a little easier to understand why the girl had come to such a religiously conservative town.

I had been walking for half an hour without coming upon either a hotel or the seafront, when an old man sitting on a little wooden stool outside a grain store called me over. His was the first greeting I had received – everyone else had ignored me as studiously as had the young men at the bus stand. Since I had by now realised that if I were to get anywhere in Tishioni I would need the help of a local contact or two, I acceded to his summons. The man sat leaning forward over his crossed legs, his elbow resting on his knee as he cradled a tiny porcelain cup of black coffee between his fingers. He wore a long white robe and a brimless white cap emblazoned with

Arabic calligraphy. His face was long and drawn and he was missing several teeth, but his eyes were warm and bright, with an expression that seemed to contain both pleasure and concern.

He pulled up another stool for me. 'We don't see people like you here anymore,' he said in French. 'Did your car break down? If you are looking for a mechanic, they are on the far side of the market.'

I told him I was looking for a hotel.

'A hotel?' he said. 'You want to stay? You must have important business. Even the missionaries are afraid to come here these days.'

'Is that because of Sharia?' I asked, although having visited cities governed by Islamic law elsewhere in Africa, I had presumed that as a Westerner and a non-Muslim I would have nothing to fear.

'Sharia is not the problem. We have had Sharia in Tishioni for years without any trouble. No, it is these young men – maybe you have seen them around.' Assuming he meant those I'd seen at the bus stand, I nodded. 'They are turning away from the true religion. They are becoming – what is it they say – radicalised?'

Far to the north of Tishioni, the old man explained over the noise of the traffic, a group had emerged that had vowed to bring down the country's secular but corrupt government and impose Sharia law nationwide. The group's interpretation of Sharia, however, was different to the version that prevailed in Tishioni and its surrounds. Christians, he said, had for many years coexisted peacefully with Tishioni's Muslim community, but Kaaba United National Terminator Squad, as the group called itself, had promised to force any Christian it encountered to convert to Islam. Those who refused would be beheaded. Women in the settlements it had conquered – the country's army, more adept at extracting bribes than fighting battles, was putting up little resistance to the group's southward push – had been forced to cover every inch of skin on their bodies. Girls had been banned from attending even the extremist schools that had survived the Islamists' purge. Alcohol, music, football and the telling of jokes were prohibited, transgressors whipped or stoned to death. It had been reported in the British press that one of the sultry socialists had joined the group, attracted by its hatred of America and capitalism and by the idea of revolution ("Mujahideen Matilda", the tabloids had nicknamed her). 'The country is going to hell,' the old man sighed.

While he spoke I noticed that many of the passers-by were stopping in their tracks to greet him, a shouted "Salaam Alaikum" followed by a slight bow of the head before they hurried on their way. He returned the greetings with a mumbled reply. Hailing a passing coffee vendor, he ordered two cups and passed one to me. When I reached into my pocket for change, he pressed down my forearm and handed the vendor a few coins. He laughed when I protested. 'You are a guest in my country,' he said, as if that sealed the argument.

As the sun sank behind the tall, tan-coloured buildings, the street began to empty out. Everybody seemed in a hurry. But this impression of bustle and purpose, the old man warned, was a product of fear, not success.

'The city is prosperous,' he said, sipping slowly at the strong, peppery coffee. 'There is money here. But there is trouble coming. I have seen this in my dreams.'

'In your dreams?' I said, surprised after his sober account of the region's recent history that he had suddenly spun off into the irrational.

'Yes, I have dreams about the future. I warn people about them. At first they do not believe me, but when they see that the dreams come true they come back to ask me what else is in store for them.' He chuckled. 'Of course they are asking the impossible - I cannot control my dreams, I just report them - but if you were not sitting here many of these people would be queuing up to seek my advice, not just greeting from afar.'

'And what have your dreams told you about Tishioni?' I asked him. Claims to clairvoyance were commonplace in these parts, and I tried not to sound too condescending.

'It is not only my dreams – anyone who wants to see knows what is coming. We are sitting in the centre of town, of course there is commerce here. But you do not have to go far from the centre to find terrible poverty. There are no jobs for the young. Herding is finished – there is no rain. The few herders who remain have to come into town to buy food for their livestock because there is no pasture left. Fishing, too, is almost finished – foreign trawlers have plundered our seas because as long as they gave big enough bribes the government let them do what they like. Even the textile industry is under threat. Our factories are closing because they cannot compete with the Chinese – the Chinese sell fabric to our women, copying our African patterns and pretending the material is home-made. What you see is the beginning of the end. Soon, Tishioni will be like one of those towns upcountry: *fini*.'

From a nearby minaret came the tinny wail of the call to prayer. People stopped what they were doing and either headed for the mosque or prepared to kneel where they stood. The old man excused himself. He removed his flip-flops and splashed water over his head, hands and feet from a plastic kettle brought out from his store by a boy. I waited while he and the boy prayed. Across the street on a petrol station forecourt, a line of men bowed in submission. I sat watching, again feeling alone.

'Those who have money know what is happening,' the man continued after regaining his stool. 'They do not need me to tell them, they are not stupid. So they cling to what they have, and hoard all the jobs and wealth. Those coming up, the young people graduating from school, have no hope. There are no jobs for them. And the elders cling to political power too, because they know that when business dries up politics will be the only way to make a living. So the young cannot do anything to change the system. But while those who have money can see that the economy is in trouble, they cannot see the danger this will bring to the city. I have tried to tell them what I have seen in my dreams. I have tried to reason with them. But they are like a sailor I once warned about rough seas. They stop up their ears. The fanatics do not come from nowhere. They join these jihads because they have no jobs and no hope, and because women and their elders do not respect them. Already, young people from Tishioni have travelled north to join the jihadists, but the people in power here refuse to believe this. They stay in their compounds by the beach – they know nothing of what is happening in the slums. They think the army and the police will protect us, that it is impossible that they will allow the city to be attacked. But when these people reach us, this Kaaba United or whatever they call themselves,' he pronounced the name with a strong French accent, 'there will be thousands of young people here ready to join them. Ordinary people know this – you see how they are rushing to get home before dark? But those in power ignore the danger. The jihadists will not need to bring a Trojan horse – their troops are already here.'

'Have they tried to attack the city?' I asked. I was thinking not just about my own safety but the girl's.

'There was a raid on a police station. Nobody was killed but they freed some prisoners and took them away. And there was a petrol bomb in the Christian quarter, in a bar. But who knows what will happen in the future? In my dreams I have seen floggings, beheadings, kidnappings. You need to be careful. That sailor ignored my warnings. He went to sea and drowned.'

I was beginning to feel anxious. 'Are the bars in the Christian quarter still open?' I asked.

'Ah, you want to go to the bars,' he smiled knowingly. 'For the women, I suppose.'

'For one woman, yes,' I admitted, not wishing this venerable figure to think I was some kind of libertine.

He drained his porcelain cup and nodded slowly. 'I know the one you mean,' he said. 'She came to me in one of my happier dreams. Her beauty is God-given. It is as if she is clothed in the sun. Her smile is as warm as African hospitality – as warm, even, as it was before the white man came. But as with our hospitality, that beauty cannot last. It will be followed by ugliness. Like those joyful visions people have in the moments before dying, her appearance in Tishioni is a portent of our doom.'

'And the bars?' I reminded him – the turn the conversation had taken disconcerted me.

'Some are still open,' he said. 'There are still a few reckless customers. Even the one that was bombed did not close down. But as I say, you need to be careful. The Hisbah have become stricter.' He was referring to the religious police force who took it upon themselves to enforce Sharia law in the city. 'They are worried they will be targeted by the jihadists if they do not show enough zeal. It will not be long before they start to clamp down on the Christians.'

I was keen after hearing what he had said to find a room before dark, so I began to take my leave. Advising me to steer clear of the Christian quarter, he told me where I could find a hotel near the sea.

'And be sure not to stay longer than necessary,' he added. 'I too will be leaving soon, inshallah.'

Out of politeness I asked him where he was going.

'To the mountains to the north, if Allah wills it,' he said, stroking the grey stubble of his chin. 'There I will study the Book of Enoch. I suppose you know of the Book of Enoch?'

'I do, but it's Christian, isn't it?' I replied (as a schoolboy cynic I'd been more interested in the books that had been expunged from the Bible than those that had stayed in, and the Book of Enoch was one of the more outlandish of these apocrypha).

'We are all People of the Book,' he said patiently. 'Enoch himself was a Jew, the great-grandfather of Noah. But his writings are for all of us, and they are of great relevance today. They talk of the Watchers, angels who fell from grace because they could not control their lust.' I looked up from my empty coffee cup to see if he was admonishing me, but his gaze was directed at the figures passing by in the darkening, traffic-lit street. 'And they talk of dream visions, visions like mine, where the fallen angels are judged and carnage and chaos are loosed upon the land. But like my dreams, the visions of Enoch were disbelieved. He knew how the world worked, he saw the end of all things, but only the Christians of the northern mountains continue to believe in what he wrote. Even though a copy of the book was found on top of the peak I hope to visit, the Jews and other Christians reject his warnings. The Book of Enoch, you understand, is not for the fainthearted.'

Out of gratitude for his hospitality I had continued to listen to him, but I was eager to be on my way and his ruminations seemed increasingly unhinged. I stood to leave and we shook hands. 'Beware of the Hisbah police,' he warned as a parting shot, 'they can make things difficult for you.'

10

I have often heard it said, not just by disillusioned aid workers and missionaries but by Africans themselves, that everybody in Africa is for sale. The rich and powerful, the argument goes, must continually shore up their position by peddling favours and influence. The poor, meanwhile, have no choice but to sell themselves to the highest bidder, even if that bidder is recruiting them for shady activities.

I've never had much truck with this argument – not, at any rate, in applying it solely to Africans. We're all for sale aren't we? I don't just mean the obvious sellouts - contestants in reality TV shows, writers of smutty novels, or sultry young beauties marrying rich old beasts. I mean the rest of us – the browbeaten wage slaves who sell every waking hour to their employers, the careerists who fawn and backstab their way to success, the journalists who would trade their mothers for a story, the bankers who turn a blind eye to their clients' crimes. Even I had to work quite hard when I was throwing parcels for a living. The ones we call prostitutes might be the least whorish of us all - at least they only sell their bodies.

That said, I have to admit that when it comes to acquiring sex in Africa, blurred is the line that separates outright prostitution from sex for favours, gifts or cash. The schoolgirl who straddles her teacher for a good grade, the married mother whose sugar-daddy neighbour keeps her in skin whitener, the waitress who will fellate you for a skewer of beef, the Minister for Women bending plump-buttocked over the president's desk – none of these women would consider themselves prostitutes, but if you have money they're yours.

This blurring, and the confusion it causes, can be expensive for the inexperienced visitor. The shy girl you meet in a bar, who refuses to leave your house in the morning until you give her a "taxi fare" home. The student you meet on a dating site, with her ambition to become a doctor so she can help her country, who coyly denies you a blowjob until you give her money to buy schoolbooks for her son. The professional woman – the aid worker, the TV presenter, the embassy receptionist - who is well-off by local standards but keeps you awake all night pestering you for a visa to Europe. None of them is in it for love.

This mercenary impulse had intensified over the years, and latterly I had stuck mainly to the obvious pros. The pros were straightforward – you knew what you were getting with them, and you knew how much it'd cost. Nor did you have to spend hours persuading them to go to bed with you, just to keep up the pretence that they weren't in it for the cash. Now and then a girl would slip through the net, and someone I thought was a professional turned out to be only a part-timer. These blunders were costly and time-consuming, but over the years my ability to spot a fake had improved.

In Tishioni this ability would be particularly useful. Here, only outright prostitution was allowed, and then only in the Christian quarter. Anything else would be punished. Even a session with a prostitute was only permitted if you were unmarried - the Quran's views on commercial sex might have been ambiguous, but the religious police came down hard on adulterers. Notwithstanding my aberration with the vigorous Valerie, I was no longer in the market for casual sex, but it was reassuring to know that if I did lapse again it would be with the genuine article, and that I wouldn't have to worry that I was transgressing the Hisbah's perverted rules.

I spent my first few days in the town lying low. I knew this increased the likelihood that I would once again miss the girl, but after the old man's warnings and the stony reception at the bus stand I decided I'd prefer to run that risk than the risk of having my head lopped off. My plan was to make a surgical strike – to find out where the girl was, home in on her, and persuade her to join me in getting out of Tishioni as quickly as possible. What I hoped for after that I wasn't sure; I no longer felt I had much influence over my future, and in this volatile part of the world only the naïve make concrete long-term plans.

I made enquiries, in and around my windblown seafront hotel. I asked about the Christian quarter, which had once lain on the outskirts of town but was now hemmed in by the vast slums where job-seeking migrants from the interior had made their homes. The European colonials who had established the district, with its churches, post office, golf course and tennis club, were long gone. After independence, the textile industry they had nurtured to raise cash for the colony had been taken over by well-educated African Christians from the south. The Africans had also moved into the Europeans' villas, where they continued the tradition of having their houseboys bring them gin and tonic to sup on the verandah as the sun went down.

Now, with the decline of textile production and the rise of Islamic fanaticism, even some of the Africans were upping sticks. A number of the Christian quarter's drinking dens, I was told, had closed, either because of Hisbah police harassment or because their owners had been scared off by the reports from the north. Others operated behind closed doors, admitting only customers they knew well. Beyond this I drew a blank – most of those I spoke to limited themselves to warning me of the perils of visiting the quarter after dark.

But amid the gloom there was one blinding ray of light. The girl was here. I could tell from the sparkle in their eyes that the townspeople must have seen her, but only the old man had been willing to talk about her, and he had beheld her in a dream. Confirmation of her presence came from an unexpected source. I was lunching on boiled chicken one afternoon in a shack by the beach when two men walked in and took seats opposite me at the establishment's only table. Grey-haired and plump, they were both wearing maroon shirts with white dog collars. Silver crucifixes hung from their necks. One of the men carried a suitcase, and when I asked what had brought them to the Muslim part of town, he explained in the old-fashioned English that was typical of his kind that he was a visiting preacher, and that his friend had come to meet him at the bus stand. 'He insisted we drop by this place for lunch,' he added, smiling.

The other man giggled. 'Mama rustles up the best chicken in Tishioni,' he said, rubbing his stomach and looking fondly at the cook's fulsome rear end as she bent washing plates over a bowl. 'It will take more than a couple of bombs to stop me partaking of her treats.'

He did not appear an especially puritanical priest, so I asked if what I'd heard about the bars in the Christian quarter was true. He nodded sombrely. 'It is true,' he said. 'The life has been draining from the area. People are afraid. And our recent arrival will only make it worse.'

'Recent arrival?' the man with the suitcase said with a snigger. 'I have been here less than an hour and already I am causing trouble?'

His host laughed again. 'You? Of course not! You will be an asset to our parish – it is a pity you are staying only for a few days. No, I refer to a young lady.' A shiver ripped through my chest and arms. 'A lady,' he almost whispered, drawing us into his naughty secret, 'of the night.'

The other man nodded knowingly, as if accustomed to reports of the degradation caused by the sex trade. 'This is what happens when we lose our grip on our Christian morals,' he said.

'No, my friend, it is not the prostitution itself that is the issue. We have had prostitutes in Tishioni for many years without any problems. It is these Hisbah police - they are destroying everything.'

The priest sighed, his forearms flat on his thighs as he waited to receive his lunch. 'When they first began to conduct their raids there was no problem,' he went on. 'Yes, a few men were flogged, but the girls simply altered their working hours to avoid the Hisbah agents and it was fine. But with this girl such discretion is impossible. Everywhere else is quiet, but any bar she works in is packed to the gunwales from morning to night. Men queue up just to catch a glimpse of her – even the Muslims. They throw caution to the wind.'

'She's working then?' I couldn't stop myself blurting out, in no doubt who he meant.

'What? Who? You know her?' The priest looked startled.

'I've heard about her,' I blustered, surprised by my lack of sang-froid. The two clerics looked at each other. The grey curtain that served as a door to the shack rippled in the breeze. Mama was crouching on her haunches, using a scrap of cardboard to fan the little charcoal cooking fire on which she was boiling a chicken in a pan.

'I am not sure if she has any customers,' the priest said. 'Her fee is very high, even for the businessmen of Tishioni. But she is a bonanza for the innkeepers. Even if she spends only a day in each bar, the money they take is more than they normally earn in years.'

'What is so special about this girl?' the visiting preacher asked, looking perplexed.

I managed to refrain from answering him myself. 'I have not seen her,' said the priest. 'It would be unseemly for me to join the throng. But they tell me she is the most beautiful woman Tishioni has ever laid eyes on. And don't forget,' he winked, 'that Tishioni has been famous since Old Testament times for the beauty of its women, ever since our Queen of Sheba breached the defences of King Solomon.'

The preacher looked thoughtful. 'And where might we find this uncommon beauty, this gift from God?' he asked.

'Gift from God?' the priest spluttered. 'More likely she is an emissary of the Devil. Her presence will be the end of the Christian quarter. As soon as they get wind of the commotion she is causing among the Muslims of the town, the terrorists will be upon us. If what they have done in the north is any indicator, they will raze our district to the ground.'

'Which bars does she go to?' I asked, my impatience again getting the better of me.

'She moves around. The Hisbah cannot arrest all the men – they do not have enough prison cells or enough flagellators to deal with so many sinners. So instead they close the bars, after having a good ogle at the girl themselves, of course.'

'Why not just arrest her?' the visiting preacher asked, eyeing me mischievously as a pang of fear shook my ribcage.

'There would be uproar,' the priest replied. 'They would be lynched. And besides, the innkeepers give them a percentage of the night's takings. No, they close down the bar, and the girl has to move to another. The innkeepers know her advent will mean the end of their business, but they are nonetheless desperate to have her. Sooner or later they will be forced to close down anyway, such is the Christian quarter's plight, but she gives them a nest egg so that they can retire in comfort.'

Mama brought the men a plate of chicken and rice to share. They tucked into it with relish, rolling gobbets of meat and rice into balls and sucking their fingertips between mouthfuls. I rose to take my leave.

91

'If you yourself are trying to catch a glimpse of her you should be careful,' the priest advised me as I handed Mama a few notes. 'You will have no trouble finding her – you need only look for the bar that has a crowd of men engulfing it. But the terrorists' noose is tightening, and the Hisbah police are eager to prove their fanatical credentials. As a white man they might wish to make an example of you. You would not want your rear end striped by a hippo-hide whip, would you?'

The two men chuckled conspiratorially as I departed. Returning to my hotel room I felt a mixture of excitement and apprehension. That I was at last in the same town as the girl was one thing, working out what to do when I met her quite another. And the circumstances in which that meeting now seemed likely to take place – crowds of men jostling to get close, the Hisbah police watching her every move, the owner of the bar blocking any attempt I might make to spirit her away to somewhere calmer – promised to be a good deal more complicated than I had envisaged.

I lay on my bed trying to make a plan, but could think of nothing more likely to succeed than my trusted old method of flashing the cash - and flashing it to the Hisbah too if necessary. History told me that relying on charm to win her round would be a reckless strategy, and she didn't sound like the kind of girl who would melt at the sight of my white skin. I was no longer fully confident that money was the answer – although encouraged to hear that she was still charging a high fee, I was still troubled by the story of her fleeing the rich politician. I had no other levers, however. If hard cash didn't work...

I got to my feet without letting the thought finish. These feelings of agitation were unfamiliar, and I was struggling to come to grips with them. A craving for sex was nothing new, but this was more acute. It might have been exhaustion, or perhaps spending so many years in the tropical heat had begun to turn my mind to jelly (this was an old affliction among Europeans in Africa - the French colonisers of West Africa had had a name for the condition, *soudanité*, and affected Gallic officials had been known to go on murderous rampages, impaling natives' heads on sticks and declaring themselves to be African chiefs before gunning down their own troops). Whatever the cause, I no longer felt in complete control of what I was doing, and I hoped I would soon get back on an even keel.

From the bucket provided by the hotel I splashed water over my face and hair. I rubbed my head down with a towel, changed my shirt and squeezed into clean trousers (I would have liked to air the sore above my knee, which was by now suppurating, but the wearing of shorts was beyond the pale in such a hardline Muslim town). Then I headed out, and made for the Christian quarter.

It was a longer and hotter walk than I'd expected. By the time I reached the first villa-lined street my shirt was soaked through and the pus from my sore was competing for pre-eminence on my trousers with large blotches of sweat. I didn't let this worry me – I'd never been foolish enough to rely on my appearance to attract women. I ran my fingers through my hair, which was as lank as kelp, and ploughed on into the district.

It was as quiet as people had said. Dusk was yielding to night, and the bustling late-afternoon crowds of the Muslim areas had given way to an eerie silence. Only a few of the villas appeared inhabited, and the dim lights glowing within them were muffled by curtains or blinds. The fronts of the little stores were shuttered. There was not a hawker or roadside market woman to be seen. With the streetlamps hanging unlit – despite Tishioni's wealth, the power supply to its Christian district was fitful - it looked like a blackout had been ordered.

Overcoming my unease, and assuming that since I hadn't seen a church I must not yet have reached the quarter's heart, I plunged further in. At length I passed a pair of bars, holes in the wall whose landlords were slumped sleeping outside in plastic chairs. With their vacant shelves and stacks of empty beer crates, neither looked like it would be able to cope with a visit from the girl. When I passed a much larger bar, now closed but distinguishable as a drinking den by the Warthog adverts on its walls, I shuddered as it occurred to me that she might have already worked her way through all the sizeable establishments and moved on.

My worry was short-lived. At a crossroads I came upon a large, unlit church. Just beyond it stood a group of people, illuminated by the glow emanating from the doorway of a low building. A spasm convulsed my chest. The crowd wasn't as large as I had been led to expect, numbering about a dozen rather than several hundred, but they were all men and all were looking in through the doorway. Most were casually dressed in shirts or T-shirts, but a few wore long robes and were rattling the prayer beads that identified them as Muslims. Their words were drowned out by the loud grind of a generator, but I could see that they were talking excitedly, with something approaching rapture on their faces.

I quickened my stride, eager to get to the girl before someone else acquired her for the night. I reached the rear of the group, my ears filled with the noise of the generator and the chatter, and jostled for a look. The men were tall, however – rangy nomads of the Sahara forced to abandon their herds for the city - and even on tiptoe all I could see was the TV screen above the bar. I elbowed my way through (none of them seemed to notice me, much less object to my pushiness), and on reaching the threshold scanned the large, low-ceilinged interior.

Groups of men were sitting at plastic tables drinking. They were talking animatedly, but I saw that each man's gaze was directed not at his companions but towards the counter off to the right. This ran the length of its side of the room, and was protected by a grille of black iron bars. Behind it slouched a stout man on a stool, his bald head framed by the snouts of two snuffling warthogs painted on the wall to his rear. Before him sat four girls. The faces of three of them, turned upwards towards the television, I could see. They were beautiful, but no lovelier than most other prostitutes I had known in Africa. The fourth sat with her back to the room. She wore a long, pale blue dress, and a matching scarf was wrapped around her head. As my eyes took in her long neck, held attentively forward as she listened to the girl beside her, I remembered the grainy photographs I'd seen on the island, and replayed in my giddy mind the writer's eulogy.

I felt my legs buckle (perhaps a touch of heatstroke – inside the bar was even hotter than outside, the feeble ceiling fan doing nothing but rearrange hot air). I gripped the back of a chair, and continued to use seat backs as a support as I picked my way between the tables. Not all the chairs, I saw with surprise, were occupied, and as that thought flitted across my mind I also briefly wondered why the girl was still here, and not writhing in the clutches of some fat tycoon. At the same time the realisation dawned that the hubbub at the tables had subsided, and that the customers, to a man, were now looking not at the girl but at me. Sweat was dripping from my eyebrows, some of it stinging my eyeballs, the rest cascading before them. My head was dizzy with the heat, with the effort to stay upright, and with the blurred image of the girl's nape, but I sensed alarm in the men's stares, consternation that someone was to take her from them. That those here could afford only to look at her didn't appear to matter – she was to be torn from their field of vision, and that would be unbearable enough.

The creak of violins blared from the TV as I drew nearer, like the soundtrack to a horror film. The three other girls watched my approach with expressions of bemused distaste, the whiteness of my skin for once failing to override the repellent effect of my drenched clothes, bulging belly and the dazed, probably somewhat deranged look in my eyes. I stumbled on, feeling on the point of passing out, reaching with both arms to support myself on the chair-backs that lined my path. Suddenly the girl, presumably wondering what was happening, turned round.

Her face was beautiful. Had she been a girl I would undoubtedly have swooned and collapsed in a blubbery heap to the floor. She was not a girl, however, but a young man, delicate-featured certainly, but with an Adam's apple protruding from the front of that shapely neck and a black tuft of beard hanging above it.

'But the girl -', I spluttered, close to collapsing anyway and forced to cling to the back of the young man's stool to stay on my feet. 'The girl? She –'. He looked at me with concern. His headscarf and robe were the uniform of the desert nomads. 'That girl has gone,' he said, knowing instantly who I meant. 'But there are others.' He smiled at the one he had been listening to, who glared back at him. The other two had turned back to the TV.

'It's OK,' I said, to the obvious relief of his companion. 'I needed to see that girl. I'm sorry – I thought –'. I was short of breath.

'Don't worry,' he said, laughing gently to assuage my embarrassment. 'Others have made the same mistake, and not all of them turn back when they realise I'm a man. But you shouldn't be here, it's dangerous for you.' His expression had turned serious. 'Why do you think everyone went quiet when they saw you? They are worried.'

'Thank you,' I said, grovelling in my embarrassment. 'Thank you. Yes, I will leave in the morning. Do you know where she's gone?'

He shook his head gravely. 'Nobody knows. She disappeared overnight. We don't even know if she is safe.'

Again I felt dizzy – the room was hotter than ever. I stumbled backwards and slumped into a chair beside one of the tables.

11

'You thought the girl was here?' On the other side of the table, behind a half-drained glass of red wine, sat a dark-skinned man with a weather-beaten face.

'Yes, I saw the crowd outside and –'.

He laughed. 'They're all here to watch the telly.' I looked round, and saw that the customers' faces were turned not towards the girls at the bar as I had thought, but towards the TV, on which contestants in an American reality show were eating yellow grubs as part of a challenge. The man laughed again as one of the contestants threw up onto the jungle floor. 'Those insects are a luxury here,' he said, 'but you whites can't keep them down.' His voice was strong and deep, his accent rustic. Despite the heat he wore a thick, long gown and a woollen hat. A small dagger hung in a sheath from his bearded neck.

'Has she been here?' I asked, beginning to feel a little calmer in my disappointment.

'If she'd been here you and I wouldn't be. The place would've been closed down. No, this place does fine without her. The landlord's still upset, though – look at him.' The stout man behind the bar was staring vacantly into space. 'He was sure she'd come here next, and if she had he'd have made so much money he could've retired. He's like one of those poor sods whose lottery ticket was one number out.'

'So you haven't seen her?' I motioned to one of the girls at the bar to bring me a beer.

'Of course I've seen her. I queued at one of the other bars for a look.' He sighed. 'I'll never see her like again – that film of tears in her eyes, as dainty as the petals of the lacewood tree in the cloud forest of Mauritius, as fragile as the forest itself. It made her look sad – I think maybe she was sad – but it was so beautiful.' His eyes momentarily glazed over. 'They cut the last two lacewood trees down you know, when they put a hotel and golf course up there.'

'Why was she sad?' I asked. None of the previous reports of her had mentioned anything about her state of mind.

'It's hard to say. I didn't get to speak to her. I knew she was out of reach so I tore myself away. But some people said she wasn't well, or that she looked tired. Probably because of the bloody landlords.'

'I thought they looked after her?'

'I'd heard that too, in other places, but not here in Tishioni. Here they didn't give her anything, not even a glass of water. They knew they'd be closed down the next day so what was the point encouraging her to come back? The Christians are like that – they hoard their money. That's why they're rich, the tight bastards. I bet that's why she moved on.'

'And you don't know where she is now?'

'Nobody does, she just left. But why are you looking for her? Were you one of the lucky ones?' he winked.

I told him wearily that I didn't know her, but that I'd been searching for her for weeks.

'And what are you going to do if you find her?' he asked. 'I hope you've got deep pockets – she's not cheap even for you whites.'

'At this rate I don't think I will find her,' I said. 'Whenever I think I've caught up with her, she disappears.'

'What's wrong with these girls anyway?' He tilted his head towards the bar, where the three women had been joined by a man with a knapsack who seemed more interested in the young nomad than in them.

'Nothing, they're beautiful,' I said. 'But this girl's different. You don't charge what she does unless you're good.' I was no longer sure either if this was the reason she charged so much or if it was why I wanted to find her, but I was feeling too drained to give thought to such questions now.

He asked where I'd heard about her. 'Oh, you've been on the island,' he smiled when I told him. 'You'll have met my friend the churchman then. He spends a lot more time in Harry's bar than in church, though. You must've come across him.'

'It was the churchman who told me about the girl,' I said, surprised that we had such a far-off acquaintance in common. 'How do you know him?'

'I used to work on the lake. We drank together. Good drinker, the churchman.'

'Likes his working girls too,' I said.

'Not just working girls,' the man chuckled. 'Other men's wives as well. Mind you, some of them are more or less prostitutes themselves – buy them a tub of skin whitener and you're in there. Did he tell you about that agent bloke from the fish factory? Our friend borrowed money from him and told him it was for repairs to the church. What he really needed it for was to pay the agent's wife for a fuck. Then after he'd had his way with her he told the bloke he'd paid the loan back to his wife, with interest!'

We both laughed. I'd given up on any notion of finding the girl tonight, and talking to this solid, grounded man was helping me to recover my equilibrium. 'What did you do on the lake?' I asked him.

'I'm a sailor. That's why I'm so dark - they call me the black man around here. I did a bit of piracy there.'

'Piracy? But there's nothing to steal, is there? The lake's dead.'

'Not now, no, but a few years ago it was booming. I worked for the fish factories, confiscating fishing gear from the local fishermen so the factories could get control of the lake.'

'Confiscating!'

'That's what they called it. They said it was better for everybody if they controlled everything. The government agreed with them because the fish they exported brought in foreign currency, so it let us take what we wanted. The only people who lost out were the locals, but nobody cared about them. I knew it was piracy, but if it hadn't been me they'd have hired someone else to do it.'

He finished his wine, and I took a cooling slug of Warthog. The contestants in the reality show were arguing over rice rations. 'Is that why you've got the dagger?' I said.

'Yeah, just in case. You never know with fishermen – they're tough bastards.' After the lake ran out of fish, he told me, he had become a marine pirate in the Indian Ocean, as a member of a team of sailors who hijacked passing container ships for ransoms. 'Good money that was, while it lasted,' he said, 'before the terrorists took it over. Bastards. But I'm out of all that now. I'm taking the Magdalene to Saudi Arabia tomorrow.'

'The Magdalene?'

'My dhow. I'm going to sail her to Jeddah, inshallah. Then I'll make my way over land to Mecca.'

'You're doing the Hajj?'

'I am,' he said proudly. 'That's why I don't mind telling you about my evil deeds.' He chuckled again. 'Soon all my sins will be paid for.'

'What's tonight then? A last blast?'

'Exactly. After the Hajj there'll be no more wine and no more women. My high living days are over. Tonight you are in attendance at an old sailor's last fling.'

I asked if he was worried about the Hisbah.

He shook his head. 'Now the girl's left there's no reason for them to hang around. The worst one's gone on an extended holiday, to spend all the money he made while she was in town. Corrupt sod. Goes on about morals and honesty, then takes bribes to let the bars stay open for another night. Then he closes them down so the terrorists'll think he's a strict enough Muslim. Clever he is, I'll give you that. But he's a bastard. Anyway, if you'll excuse me,' he pushed his chair back as he rose, 'I have business to attend to.' He looked towards the bar. 'Feel free to join me.'

I declined, and he went over to the three girls. The young nomad had gone, and the man with the knapsack watched while the sailor and the girls talked. I noticed with resignation that they showed a great deal more interest in the seaman than they had in me, and it was not long before he had one of them – a buxom young beauty with big curls, pale brown skin and bright red lipstick - sitting sideways on his lap, her stockinged legs draped across his thighs as he cupped his callused hand on one of her buttocks. After a few minutes he lowered her to her feet. Winking smugly at the man with the knapsack, who had looked up from the message he was typing on his phone, he led her off by the hand. He waved as they passed my table. As I watched her swaying rear end I was surprised to feel not the slightest twinge of envy.

I had begun to ruminate on the possible reasons for this unusual absence of sensation when there was a commotion at the doorway. I looked up to see a tangle of flailing limbs as the sailor's thick forearms struggled to free themselves from the grip of two brawny, white-robed men. 'Leave me alone you bastards!' he was shouting as he tried in vain to elbow them both in the ribs. 'I'm not married! There's nothing about this in the Quran! Don't forbid yourselves the good things, it says. You're not just hypocrites, you're ignorant!' His torso strained and twisted, his still-sheathed dagger swinging wildly below his chin. As they subjugated his upper body he kicked at their shins, only to find that his legs had become ensnared in the folds of his gown. 'Bastards!' he shouted again. The men forced his arms behind his back and pushed him kicking and shouting out to the street. As his receding shouts were snuffed out by the slam of a car door, followed quickly by the throaty gunning of an engine, his companion adjusted her skirt and walked back to the bar as if nothing had happened.

Shaken by this spectacle, I decided it was time to leave, but in my flustered state I hadn't made a plan for getting back to my hotel late at night. The chance of finding a taxi appeared slim, and walking alone at this hour would be asking for trouble. Without much hope I approached the bar and asked the landlord if he could call me a cab. 'Where are you going?' the man with the knapsack interrupted. 'I can give you a lift if it's not too far.' The landlord turned back to the TV. I told the man where I was staying. 'That's good, I can take you. It's on my way. Just let me reply to this message and we'll go.' He typed something into his smartphone. His eyes were shiny and slightly feverish, the skin of his face as smooth as a bottletop. He had a mop of bleached blond hair squashed in under his baseball cap, on the front of which was a picture of Christ in a Muslim turban holding a Quran. He led me out to his car, a brand new Chinese hatchback. He stashed his knapsack on the back seat and we drove off.

'What will they do to him?' I asked, still unnerved by what had happened to the sailor.

'He will be flogged,' he bleated. There was a look of satisfaction in his eyes. His voice was high and goat-like. 'That's what happens to you if you use prostitutes, or if you indulge in the other vices. That man is a glutton, he wants it all. And on top of that his tongue is a cesspit. You heard him, didn't you? He is a flagrant sinner. Flogging is the least he deserves.'

It was futile to argue. We drove slowly through the darkened, empty streets. The man sat hunched over the steering wheel, gripping it tightly with both hands. His little eyes flitted between the road ahead and me, as if he was afraid I would attack him. Whenever he reached down to change gear the car veered across the road, careering towards the lifeless buildings. He would regain control just in time to set us back on course.

'And what were you yourself doing in such a den of vice?' he said suddenly, a sly smile creasing his face.

'I was looking for a friend,' I said.

'That man is your friend?' He raised his eyebrows, affecting shock.

'Not him, no, I only met him tonight.'

'Then I think you are talking about a girl.' He nodded smugly to himself, and without waiting for my confirmation went on. 'You too are a glutton, I see. An imbiber of liquor and a consumer of prostitutes. It is to be expected, of course - you are a Christian.'

'I'm not looking for her to consume her,' I replied. In the headlights a goat flashed across our path - he braked sharply to avoid hitting it.

'She is a whore!' he whinnied. 'What else will you do with her? Ask for her hand in marriage?' He changed gear violently and we swerved towards the drainage ditch that flanked the road.

'She is not just any prostitute,' I said as he wrenched us back on track. 'She –'

'Indeed she is not! She is a witch! Her beauty is a trap. It lures the weak. That behind of hers …' The fury went out of his stare, and his grip on the wheel loosened. Again we drifted ditchwards. 'It is as pliable as those young men who joined up with the terrorists and blew themselves up.' He regained control. 'But she is a demon! She sucks you in and spits you out. Even you whites can't afford her.' His brow clenched in a scowl. 'So you too have been bewitched.'

'I just want to find out what all the fuss is about,' I protested. Since the episode with the nomad a constricted feeling had set in below my throat, and the words came out with difficulty. He shook his head quickly, still gripping the wheel, but did not speak. The streets showed no sign of life; there wasn't so much as a burning pile of rubbish to indicate any recent human presence. The ride back to the hotel was taking longer than I had anticipated, and I began to doubt whether the man really knew where I wanted to go.

'You know where my hotel is, don't you?' I said.

His vehement gaze swivelled from the road to me. 'Of course I know. In a few minutes we will arrive.' We turned a corner and came out on the seafront. 'You see?' he said. 'Your hotel is by the sea, yes?'

I nodded, and began to think about what I would do next. I knew I had to get out of Tishioni, but I had no leads as to where the girl had gone. I decided my only option was to head for Umfiki, an equally large but reportedly much less forbidding city a few hours down the coast, and hope either that the girl had had the same idea or, if not, that its inhabitants would know of her whereabouts. I recalled the young nomad's allusion to her safety, and a sharp pain rattled my forehead - what if something had happened to her, if the fanatics or someone else had got hold of her? But there was nothing I could do about that, I told myself – as so often in Africa, I would have to put my trust in fate.

These thoughts were cut short by an abrupt reminder of fate's fickleness. The driver had taken a sudden turn off the seafront. Before I could ask what was happening, he had stopped the car in a narrow lane outside a small building. Two men ran towards us. They pulled open my door and hauled me out roughly by the arms. I recognised them as the men who had apprehended the sailor. 'What's this about?' I shouted as they bundled me towards the building. 'What have I done?' I managed to look over my shoulder, and saw the driver still sitting at his wheel, staring fixedly ahead.

'Just come with us,' one of the men said gruffly, 'and you'll be fine.'

I wasn't reassured. As a white man in Africa I generally felt safe from violence at the hands of the authorities – in most places it was too much hassle for the police or army to rough you up and risk a diplomatic incident – but these Islamic fanatics were a different matter. For them, a flogged white man would be a badge of honour, a recruiting tool. The Hisbah police, as I had seen with the sailor, could make up their own rules. The only people they had to fear were even more deranged than they were, and would no doubt approve of their shredding of infidel flesh.

I was shoved through the door of the building into a bare room with a single dim lightbulb hanging from the ceiling. In the far corner, bound tightly to a chair, sat the sailor, champing at the gag they had tied around his mouth. Behind a wooden table in the middle of the room sat a man I hadn't seen before. He wore a white turban, although it was not this that held the eye but his extraordinary face. Most people in these parts had light-brown skin, the skin of desert-dwellers who kept their faces shielded from the sun and derided Africans from farther south for their blackness. But this man's face was a burnt red colour, like some southern European peasant who had drunk too much wine in his life. Not all of it was red, however – his brow under his turban was black and scabby, and his cheeks and lightly-bearded chin were covered in huge white boils. One or two of the boils appeared to be on the point of exploding; others seemed to grow as you stared at them. It was like looking at the frothing surface of an incandescent planet.

The two men stood me in front of him, gripping my upper arms. The sailor writhed and grunted in his corner. The air in the room was sweltering.

'You know why you are here?' the man said, looking up at me, in a voice whose calmness was a stark contrast to the frenzy on his face.

'I can guess,' I said. I was confident he would accept a bribe in return for my freedom, and didn't want to aggravate him by protesting my innocence.

'You have been consorting with harlots. Just like this man,' he motioned with his chin to the sailor, 'you are a glutton and a sinner.'

I rejected the accusation, although I knew it was pointless to try to reason with him.

He snorted. 'You have been pursuing a whore across Africa,' he said, his voice still calm. 'A beautiful whore, I admit - her breasts were as firm as the click of the bushman's tongue, before those godless pagans finally disappeared from the face of the earth - but a whore nevertheless. There is no point in denying it – I have it on good authority.' He looked over my shoulder, and when I followed his gaze I saw the blond driver standing behind me, slyly triumphant.

'You're the one I heard about then,' I couldn't help saying.

'You heard about me?' A frown began to crumple his scabby black brow.

When I mentioned Hubert's name, his glower solidified. He rose slowly to his feet and moved round the table to stand before me.

'And you believe that fraud?' he said, his voice growing louder. 'That fraud who will trick the freshly bereaved into emptying their pockets so that he will pray for their dead?' He was trembling with anger. As he leaned towards me I thought I caught a whiff of alcohol on his breath.

'I'm just saying what I heard,' I replied. I had begun to sweat more profusely; my plan to humour him was going awry.

He nodded at the two men, and their grip on my arms tightened. 'Tomorrow, while this man is being flogged,' he said, 'you will be on your way to the north.'

I gulped. 'The north?' I said weakly, my constricted throat suddenly dry as dust.

106

'You know about Kaaba United National Terminator Squad,' he said, still leaning close to my face. 'They can make a lot of money out of someone like you. And we can make a lot of money handing you over to them.'

'But I'm from Britain,' I said, straining to push the words out. Although I was still hoping to bribe him, it dawned on me that he could make more money by selling me to the fanatics. I couldn't keep from my mind the hackneyed image of a hooded man with a sword looming over a kneeling hostage (or perhaps it would be Mujahideen Matilda, who would no doubt be delighted to finish me off). 'The British government doesn't pay ransoms to terrorists,' I whined.

This was true – while other European governments coughed up millions to free kidnapped citizens from crazed Islamists, the British Foreign Office believed that such payments only fortified the terror groups and increased their capacity to carry out attacks.

The man was unmoved. 'Well, it will be up to them to decide what to do with you. We will merely deliver you into their custody. We have spoken to our friends in the group already. They did not object to receiving a Britisher.' The sailor's grunts grew louder – he was glaring at me, as if he wanted to tell me something through his gag. When I looked at him his pupils swivelled to one side. I followed his gaze, and through a small window to my left saw two figures standing outside in the darkness. The figures were wearing hoods. I gulped so deeply I almost retched.

'Take him to the car,' the planet-faced Hisbah officer told his henchmen.

'Wait, can't we negotiate?' I had expected him to ask me for money, but seeing how steadfast he was I began to panic. Again my legs felt weak, and I slumped a little in the two men's grip.

'Negotiate? Why do you need to negotiate if you are British? Surely you have nothing to fear. Will they not release you as soon as they see your passport?' He sniggered. 'Take him,' he ordered his henchmen.

They rammed their arms under my shoulders, and almost lifted me off the floor.

'I have money,' I shouted, my heart beating fast. My sweat had become a torrent.

'We don't want your money!' His face was redder than ever. 'We will get enough money from the jihadists!'

The men turned me towards the door and pushed me forward. The sailor was still grunting loudly behind me. The weasel-eyed driver sneered under his baseball cap as I was shoved past him. I saw through the open door of the building that another vehicle, a black Land Cruiser with tinted windows, was parked beside his. The two hooded figures were standing on either side of it, waiting. One of them, I noticed with a new shudder of alarm, had the bearing of a woman. As we approached the threshold I made a last-ditch attempt to elbow my gaolers aside and free my arms from their grasp. One of the men stumbled, and in his surprise the other loosened his grip. I lunged towards the doorway, but no sooner had my head and torso emerged into the open air than I fell forward, flat on my face. The blond driver had stuck out a leg to trip me, and the two henchmen dived onto my back as I lay on the ground.

'Get him up,' the Hisbah officer shouted. 'Put him in the car.' The men lifted me to my feet, and the two hooded figures came forward to help them bundle me towards the vehicle. I was giddy and confused, my mouth and nostrils full of dust, and they had no trouble pushing me onto the back seat. The hooded woman climbed into the driver's seat. The man sat beside me, his dark hands hastily binding my wrists with rope. Pendants showing white-clad sheikhs and scenes from Mecca hung from the rear-view mirror. On the floor in front of the passenger seat I saw through the fog that had clouded my eyes a flash of silver – a sword perhaps, or a machete. The woman turned the key in the ignition. The henchmen stepped back. With a jerk the car began to reverse, jolting me out of my torpor. Recognising with something approaching terror the bleakness of my prospects, I mustered the strength to try one last gambit.

'I have dollars!' I croaked, dust mixed with saliva dribbling from my lips.

'Stop!' the hooded man told the woman.

The reversing car bounced to a halt. The man lowered the blackened window beside him and with a shout relayed what I had said to the Hisbah officer.

'Dollars?' the officer said, striding quickly towards us.

'Yes, dollars,' I shouted across my captor, who had let go of the rope.

At a signal from the officer, the hooded man climbed down to let me out of the car. Exhausted, I stood leaning against the passenger door.

'How much do you have?' the officer asked. His voice was calm, but his narrow eyes gleamed with satisfaction beneath their swollen lids - no Islamist could resist the lure of the heathen enemy's currency.

It was futile to lie - his men could easily search me – so I told him.

'I see.' He leaned towards me. His boils were palpitating, and I drew my head back lest one of them burst. 'That will be a useful addition to the funds for our trip, will it not?' He took a step back and smiled at the blond driver, who had come up behind him.

'My friend and I,' he continued as the driver placed his knapsack on the car's bonnet, 'have been doing good business because of your whore. It is a shame she has left us, but we are going on a little journey, inshallah, to celebrate her time in Tishioni.'

'I was told you'd already gone,' I said, glancing towards the building where the sailor had by now ceased his writhing.

'We will leave tomorrow, after we attend to our naval friend. After so many nights of depravity he no longer has the means to pay us the fine that would buy him his freedom. We are off to visit a great mosque in the centre of Africa, built by two of our continent's greatest Islamic leaders. And we will put your dollars to good use - they will enable us to fulfil our duty, as Muslims, to give alms to the poor.' From inside the Land Cruiser behind me I heard the sound of a man chuckling – the other hooded figure was not Mujahideen Matilda after all, but my second gender mixup of the evening.

'Inshallah,' said his accomplice.

'Inshallah,' he repeated. 'But first we shall stop in Umfiki, where we have a little business to attend to. So, where is the money?'

I reached into my trouser pockets and handed over all I had. The driver counted it, his beady eyes flitting between the notes and his Hisbah companion. Then he counted it again, with a fervour that made it obvious the story about their Kaaba United connections was a fabrication. When he finished he took a chit of paper from his knapsack. He wrote on it and gave it to me: a receipt.

'Well,' the Hisbah officer said, looking relaxed as he stuffed the notes into the folds of his white cloak, 'my friend will take you home now.' He strolled back towards the building with his henchmen and the two men in hoods. His goat-faced friend drove me to my hotel.

The next morning I rose at dawn to walk to the bus stand. Not far from the hotel I came upon a crowd of robed men standing in a dusty clearing between buildings. Peering over shoulders I saw the sailor kneeling on the ground. He was half-naked, his sturdy, dark torso sweating in the rapidly-intensifying heat. His hands were bound before him. Behind him stood the Hisbah officer, who held a thick whip out in front of his chest like the conductor of an orchestra. He was lecturing the crowd about the evils of prostitution, which he described as a filthy Western import. A few of the spectators were nodding in agreement, but most weren't listening. Instead they stood on tiptoe, craning their necks and jostling to catch a glimpse of the hapless seafarer. They muttered impatiently, keen for the action to begin. As at the bar the night before, I too had to stand on tiptoe to watch. I spotted the miller at the front of the crowd to one side, grinning. He caught my eye and winked.

After a few minutes the sermon ended, and the officer moved closer to the sailor's bare, fleshy back. The crowd surged forward, and the mutterings became shouts as a few spectators near the front lost their footing and fell forward into the makeshift amphitheatre. The officer waited while they got to their feet. The sailor had hunched his shoulders and was grimacing as he waited for the first blow. The officer moved to stand by his victim's side, showing him the whip. The sailor looked up at him, failing to hide the anxiety in his eyes. The sun pounded on our heads. The crowd had begun to roar.

The whip was raised, high above the officer's turbaned head. The sailor's body tensed, the veins in his forearms and chest visible even from my position at the rear of the crowd. My own shoulders hunched in empathy, but I had no wish either to observe his torment or to attract the attention of the Hisbah, so as the cheers rang out from the crowd I sloped off, and continued on my way to the bus stand.

12

Although I had no strong reason to think I would find the girl there, it was a relief to arrive the following day in Umfiki.

By all accounts it was a city on the up. The recent discovery of natural gas offshore and its proximity to one of Africa's last remaining wildlife parks gave it a whiff of excitement and energy that the places I'd passed through on my way here had lacked. The town and its environs had attracted a cosmopolitan crowd – there were British expats working at the gas plant, Chinese construction workers building a shopping mall, tourists from Europe on their way to the safari park, and American hunters proving their manliness by shooting animals. For most of the past few months I had been the only foreigner for miles around, and it was refreshing to be anonymous again.

It was refreshing, too, after the oppressive atmosphere of Tishioni, to be somewhere less uptight. For Umfiki's vitality was not without its sordid side. Chinese builders had been caught smuggling ivory from the game reserve. British gas workers had been confined to their compound, their company fearful that its multi-billion-dollar contract would be cancelled after one too many drunken rampages in town. Neither the American hunters nor the European safari-goers, meanwhile, could resist the town's many drinking establishments and the temptations therein. For some, unable to tear themselves away from the lissom young women (and men) who had come here from all over Africa to service them, the brothel cat was the wildest animal they'd see.

You might be surprised to hear about these young men. They were here to service not other men – only the reckless, and the braver American hunters, risk gay sex in Africa – but women. A booming sex tourism industry had sprung up in the town, providing solace to middle-aged European housewives and divorcees who for a couple of weeks a year escaped their shrivelled lives back home to hook up with well-endowed young Africans. The women got rugged sex and fake romance, the young Africans credit for their phones.

It is easy to judge these women, to chastise them for their seediness or for taking advantage of the wealth divide to acquire sex of a calibre they could never hope for in Europe. But who can blame them? They're no different to the businessmen, aid workers, journalists, diplomats and male tourists who indulge in a bit of extra-curricular activity on their travels. What would I get if I was back in Britain now? In my forties, overweight, leaking pus from the sore on my leg, not wealthy by European standards: all I'd get is damaged goods. And these women are the same - they'd get the likes of me, and you only have to watch them assiduously ignoring every white man who crosses their path to see how appealing they find that prospect.

And what of the young men? They too, with their lack of compunction and their fondness for marijuana and alcohol, are often criticised by their elders. They are a disgrace to their continent, they complain, a symbol of its decay. But young men here, as the old grain merchant in Tishioni had pointed out, have no other way of making a living – there are too many of them, and not enough jobs. Even having sex with milk bottles, as the white women are nicknamed, beats scratching around in the exhausted fields to grow enough to eat.

I arrived in Umfiki in the limpid light of the late afternoon, and checked in to a smart hotel by the beach. After my traumatic time in Tishioni I needed a break, and it was good to be back in air-conditioned surroundings. Prior to my sacking I had been a regular guest of Africa's best hotels, and being forced to cut down on cocktails by the pool, Asian massages and breakfast buffets the size of football pitches was one of the downsides of being laid off. Like all NGOs and government aid agencies, Feed Africa Today had been lavish with its travel expenses, using only the most exclusive chauffeur companies and the swishest hotels. To justify this to their funders they cited the threat of fraud. There were too many instances, they explained, of locally-engaged staff cooking up deals to give such business to their cousins. If they were to ensure that everything was above-board, and thereby forestall tabloid accusations that they were abetting corruption, they had no choice but to use expensive, internationally-renowned firms rather than cheaper local outfits.

This time I was paying for myself, but although my finances were less robust than they had been, there was no need to panic. I still had a few shillings of local currency, which I had left in the hotel while reconnoitring Tishioni, and I had Hubert's diamond, stored safely about my person, if the cash ran out. I decided to take my time in this attractive and friendly town, and to spend a few days regrouping while I tried to ascertain the girl's whereabouts.

It was a good place to relax. There were restaurants whose menu extended beyond lumps of cornmeal, enough drinking dens to satisfy the most dedicated bar-crawler, and an array of beautiful girls from every corner of Africa. There were statuesque Somalis, sassy Senegalese, haughty Ethiopians and upright Rwandans. There were knowing Nigerians, pert-rumped Tanzanians, guileless Ghanaians and comely Congolese. For a foreigner with no ties and a bit of money to spare, it was paradise. I half-wished I was still in the market myself.

Those days, however, were behind me. I had strayed only a couple of times in the last few months, and one of those was the renewal of an old relationship. Two women in three months (or was it three women?) was celibate by average expat standards. Some aid workers I'd known had had a different girl every night of the week (I myself had never been fit enough for such exertions). One, a Spaniard who would give a girl a tip if she "sucked well", secured a steady stream of partners by paying the women he met through the dating app on his phone to give him a review that emphasised his generosity. Another, a Frenchman, worked for an international famine relief organisation that banned sexual relations with *any* locals, not just those it was saving. He had had to pay his security guard, who was contracted by his employer, to keep his nocturnal trysts quiet. When the trysts became more frequent, they agreed a flat monthly rate for the guard's discretion.

It wasn't that I would have felt guilty if I'd continued to indulge (in Valerie's case I'd probably have felt more guilty if I hadn't), but keeping myself in as good shape as possible for when I finally found the girl seemed to give me purpose, and my search for her anyway left little space in my head for thoughts of other women. It wasn't about morals or some kind of self-purifying mission – I simply wasn't as interested anymore.

Or at least, not when I was sober. There was one establishment in Umfiki that surpassed all others in the profundity and breadth of its temptations. Few tourists, big game hunters, construction workers or, before they were confined to their luxury compound, gas company employees could resist its lures. A night out anywhere else would invariably end in a visit here. In its short existence, this den of sensuality had acquired a fame that almost rivalled that of the girl.

The haven in question was a bathhouse. Bathhouses were common in North Africa, but virtually unheard-of south of the Sahara. This one, decked out in marble and soaring arches like the most opulent Turkish hammam, had been erected by a local businesswoman who had come across the concept during a pilgrimage to Jerusalem. But although this Christian entrepreneur had spared no expense in mimicking the décor of the baths she'd seen in the Middle East, she had radically distorted the normal function of such places. Her baths, which she had named, simply, Moisture, were less about getting clean than getting dirty. Yes, there were bubbling pools, steam rooms, showers and saunas. There were fat women in thin towels and hairy men in loincloths. There were bars of soap, coarse gloves and pitchers of water. But none of these amenities was put to any use that your average Arab might recognise. Instead, they were diverted to erotic purposes, and clients were lubricated further by a supply of alcoholic beverages undreamt-of in baths anywhere else.

I too ended up here. I was confident that it would be the best place in town to glean information about the girl, and I felt that a few languid evenings supping Warthog while chatting to scantily-clad women (you didn't have to have sex – the bar area was sumptuously comfortable) would help reinvigorate me after the travails of Tishioni.

On my seventh night I met the owner. A large, dark-skinned woman in red fishnet stockings, expensive-looking leather shoes and a heavy scarlet headdress similar to the type worn by Ottoman sultans, she came into the bar and introduced herself. Her name was Mama Alison. Although she had clearly seen better days she was still attractive, with firm but fleshy lips, large, salacious eyes, and bounteous buttocks bulging under a tight black skirt. I was sitting on the cushioned bench that ran around the barroom's walls, a bottle of chilled Warthog on the table before me. Without asking, she slid in next to me, settling with her hip up against mine. The cushions, covered in purple velvet, were thick and soft. Brass lamps in the Moroccan style hung from the low ceiling, their red bulbs giving off the dimmest of glows. In one corner an uncovered bulb hanging above the drinks display cabinet afforded a slightly brighter light to the bartender, a short man in a white shirt and bowtie who stood attentively behind his counter. Soukous music was playing at low volume. In the deep shadows around the edge of the room, rasta boys ran their fingertips over doughy white thighs while the painted lips of smooth-skinned beauties whispered into hairy pink ears.

'How do you like my Moisture?' the woman asked me, her saucy smile revealing a wide gap between her front teeth.

I told her it was great, and that I wished I'd discovered it when I was younger.

'Youth is in the mind,' she laughed, slapping me on the thigh (I had on my white shorts again, to give the sore some air). She motioned towards the shadows. 'For the girls here you are a young man. Even for me,' she winked, 'if you still have the spunk, then I still have the juice.'

I laughed, but told her, not without a little residual reluctance, that I wasn't in the market.

'We are all in the market,' she said, her amused voice loud and hearty. 'Look at me. I have been through five husbands – and when I say been through I mean it: morning and night every day. But still I would take a sixth. Where did God say we have to be virgins? If you're strong enough, even you might fit the bill,' she chortled, butting me firmly with her hip.

The barman brought over a bottle of cassava gin and a carton of mango juice. He filled Mama Alison's glass with the gin, added a dash of juice and rested the bottle on its side on the table.

'I doubt I am strong enough,' I said wearily.

'Sorry? I didn't hear you.' She cupped her hand behind her ear and moved it closer to my mouth. I repeated my lament.

'You're just here for the drinks then? You must be a wealthy man.' With her hand she squeezed my thigh, close to my crotch. 'There are much cheaper places in Umfiki to get a beer.'

'I need a rest,' I said. 'And I'm looking for information.'

She sat back and shook her head with a knowing smile. 'Ah, you're a journalist. Or is it a writer? Your kind love to come here to conduct research.' She winked again. 'I'll give you credit – you are very hands-on in your investigations.'

I explained about the girl – if anyone here might know about her, I thought, it would be her.

She crossed her legs, her skirt riding high up her fulsome thighs. Unable to avoid glancing down at her taut red stockings, I took a deep breath.

'I too have seen her,' she said, prompting a flutter in my chest, 'but not here.' The flutter subsided. 'I visited her in Tishioni. Such an ugly, arid place, but such a very beautiful girl. You appear to think my legs are alluring.' With her fingers she adjusted the hem of her skirt a couple of inches upwards, revealing yet more luxuriant flesh. 'My husbands, too, went crazy for my legs. But hers were the loveliest I've seen. They were not fleshy like mine, but lithe, so lithe she seemed to glide when she walked. She was as light on her feet as a cheetah – you are old enough to remember cheetahs, are you not?' I nodded. 'She was different to the rest of us. I am not certain she was of this world.'

'Why did you go there?' I asked, surprised that even a woman would travel a long distance to see her.

'Many people went from here,' she said, taking a gulp of gin. 'Hundreds of them. Her presence in Tishioni had a negative effect on my business in Umfiki, would you believe? But in my case it wasn't lust that drew me, nor curiosity - although I must admit I was curious. No, I thought I might recruit her for my Moisture.'

'A good idea,' I acknowledged.

'Yes, it would have been good for both of us. Good for my business – although as you see, my business is doing quite well - and good for her.'

'Wouldn't she be too expensive?' I asked.

'Oh I'm sure we could have agreed a fair price, and if not, her presence here would have enabled me to increase the prices of all the other things I offer. But it wasn't only about business. We successful women need to stick together – there are few of us in Africa, as you know. I could have helped her.'

She sipped more thoughtfully at her drink.

'I think she would have benefited from my help,' she went on. 'She seemed unwell. Or at least, unhappy.' The flutter in my chest had become a deadweight. 'Although she made them fortunes, I don't think the landlords of Tishioni's bars were treating her well. The other girls were good to her – she was kind to them and helped them whenever they had problems - but the landlords were taking advantage of her.'

'Sexually?' I said, alarmed by this fresh bit of bad news.

'I don't know about that, but they were not looking after her. We women don't like to be exploited, we like to be on top. Just ask my husbands.' She grinned, but quickly regained her serious expression. 'They weren't keeping their side of the bargain. Maybe they were violent, or maybe they simply weren't giving her anything to eat or a bed to sleep in. I don't know, but she looked somehow tired and frail. She would have been treated much better here.'

'But she wouldn't come?' I waved at the barman to bring me another beer.

'She would not. She said that maybe one day in the future she would come, but that after Tishioni she had plans to go elsewhere. She wouldn't tell me where.'

'And she's not in Umfiki now?'

'Not as far as I know. Although perhaps you have heard otherwise?' She looked at me shrewdly.

'I haven't, but I've only been here a week.' The barman brought the beer, and I ordered a sachet of sugar cane gin to accompany it.

'What makes you think you can afford her anyway?' she asked with a mocking smile. 'Even the tycoons of Tishioni balked at her fee. Are you wealthier than they?'

I had been thinking the same thing, and not just since my fleecing in Tishioni - that after coming all this way I might not be able to afford her, that the top-of-the-range sex I'd dreamed of for months might be out of reach. I wasn't yet seriously concerned – everyone had a price, and she probably hadn't been offered enough money. And I had other advantages as well as my relative wealth. Local fat cats, worried about their reputations as good Christians or Muslims, wouldn't be interested in consorting with a prostitute - even the most beautiful prostitute in Africa - for more than a few nights. A middle-aged white man, on the other hand, who couldn't afford such scruples, might take such a girl on permanently, either as a mistress during his visits to the country or as a girlfriend or wife if he lived out here. If she really struck lucky, he might take her back with him to the promised lands of the West. No local man, however rich, could offer that possibility.

'I've come too far to give up now,' I said. 'I'll worry about the financials later, but if I don't find her I'll never know.'

I had been feeling more optimistic about my quest after a few nights in Moisture, but this latest conversation was a setback. As Mama Alison moved off to do the rounds of her club, I realised that Umfiki's most likely source of information on the girl not only had no more knowledge than I did of where she might have gone, but had also given me yet more bad news about her. The sailor in Tishioni had told me the girl was melancholy; now Mama Alison had said she was ill, and might have been abused. This was not something I'd bargained for. I had expected to find the girl in her prime, at the peak of her powers, but now it seemed that she, like me, might be flagging, that it was all becoming too much.

But this vulnerability, this sense that she was being worn down by the world, only added to her allure. She hinted at something

120

precious, something antique. Like a fleeting view in the rainforest gloom of some diaphanous-winged butterfly last seen before the colonisers came and long thought extinct, the reports of her had stirred something in the slough of my soul. I didn't know what it was – it wasn't a feeling I was familiar with. I knew only that the whole pursuit was beginning to unsettle me.

I ordered another Warthog and some more gin, then another. Ensconced amid the puffed-up purple cushions, my view of the rest of the room was growing hazy. Thoughts of the girl, too, grew cloudier, gradually receding into a listless blur. At length they were usurped by the image of another girl, materialising among the cushions beside me. Young and fresh-skinned, she had on a tiny pair of hotpants. Her thighs, less fleshy than those of Mama Alison, were nonetheless mouth-wateringly smooth and succulent (an extravagant contrast, I noticed as I looked down, to my own pasty pins). Before I could begin to take in the rest of her I felt her tongue in my ear. It was licking with a soft finesse that promised so much that I was unable to resist reaching over with both hands to caress her thighs. When I turned towards her, her tongue slid round into my still-gaping mouth. She kissed me as if I were a long-lost lover. As I kneaded her loins, and as the alcohol cloaked me in a gentle, wafting numbness, I felt a sense of release from the cares and hardships of the past few weeks, and a euphoric appreciation of Umfiki's hedonistic charms.

It was only when I began to tell myself that I could stay here forever, and to wonder why such a notion hadn't occurred to me before, that I remembered the girl. At first I tried to put the thought out of my mind – my new companion was stroking my ebullient groin with a professionalism that belied her years – but it was insistent. Reluctantly I undocked my mouth from the girl's. Yet more reluctantly I removed my fevered palms from her thighs. As I explained that I couldn't go on, a look of shock dilated her pretty face (I too could hardly believe what I was saying). On recovering her composure she demanded I buy her a beer as compensation. I ordered another for myself, to lower my temperature.

The following evening I went back. Buoyed by the resolve with which I had staved off the previous night's offensive, I could see no reason not to return for a beer or two. I settled into the cushioned seat and ordered my usual. Knowing that I was unlikely to have many more nights in the comfort of Mama Alison's emporium, I tempered the Warthog with a little more cassava gin than was my habit, and after a couple of hours I was again satisfyingly drunk. Mama Alison came by briefly to ask how I was. The young girl in the hotpants waved at me from the other side of the room, where she was entertaining a safari type in khakis. Otherwise I was happy with my glass for company, contentedly replenishing my energies for the task ahead.

After an interval of indeterminate length, two men appeared in the mist of my field of vision. They were standing on the opposite side of my table. As they looked down at me, their bodies shook with mirth. One of the men, I noticed with a vague feeling of unease, was in white robes; the other wore a baseball cap. Slowly they solidified into the Hisbah officer from Tishioni and his blond accomplice. Behind them in the darkness lurked three women, whose youthful loveliness was obvious even to someone in my inebriated state.

'What a pleasant surprise to see you here,' the blond man was sniggering. 'We didn't think you had any money left.'

I grunted.

'That must be why he is sitting in here by himself,' said the other. 'He can't afford a woman.' The Hisbah officer's boils seemed to have coalesced into two or three large bubbles. He shouted to the barman to bring me another drink. 'This one is on us,' he smirked. 'You cannot say we Hisbah do not fulfil our Muslim duty of giving alms to the poor.' His accomplice laughed, and they moved off with the women to sit in the far corner of the room.

I took a sip of beer and wished they hadn't ordered me another. Images from the previous night – not just of the young girl but also of Mama Alison's thighs – had begun to push more serious thought processes to the back of my mind. Mama Alison's red stockings and the squares of creamy flesh crying out to be fondled began to swirl around my head. The gin and the beer imbued them with an aphrodisiac quality, and when one of the women who had been sitting with the Hisbah men came over and straddled me I was helpless to resist. More beautiful even than last night's enticement, she too was wearing fishnet stockings, and while her glossy thighs lacked the plumpness of Mama Alison's, their tight grip on my haunches suggested that what she lacked in heft she would more than make up for in enthusiasm. I wiped the saliva from my chin and looked her up and down. Her firm breasts were standing to attention under a tight white vest. Her plaited hair extensions were tied back, her cheekbones high and prominent, the skin of her face the colour of beer. Her tongue played slowly on her soft upper lip as her deep, dark eyes gazed meaningfully into my pale, shallow ones.

My happy gawking was interrupted by the blond man in the baseball cap, who had come back over to my table. 'She is on us too,' he said with a grin. 'My friend was feeling sorry for you, sitting here on your own.' I looked over to the Hisbah officer's table, and in the shadows made out a white sleeve raising a glass of what looked like red wine in my direction.

After that I don't remember much. There are fuzzy pictures in my head of knowing looks from the hotel doorman and the pretty receptionist, of a clumsy clench in the lift, of the woman's head bobbing below my beer gut as I fumbled with the key to my room. Then it goes blank, until the following morning when I awoke with the sun blazing in my face and an anvil apparently clanking around in my head.

The young woman, to my surprise, was still there. Dressed, and looking only a little the worse for wear, she was sitting cross-legged on a chair, framed by the dazzling brightness of the window. In her hand was a folded sheet of paper.

'Your invoice,' she said calmly.

'My invoice,' I managed to say. The sheet underneath me was damp, and for some reason there was a pillow squashed below my naked buttocks. The air-conditioning unit was whirring quietly, and I pulled a sheet over my pallid paunch. 'My invoice? But -' I remembered the Hisbah officer, and sighed deeply as it dawned on me that he had tricked me again. 'Let me see it,' I said.

The paper was a pale pink colour. Below its header – the bold, baroque lettering of the Moisture logo – was a neatly-printed list of services rendered. Each succinctly-described sexual event was flanked by one box in which the woman had written the number of times it had occurred, and another where she had written the total cost of each service. In the box next to the word Fellatio, for example, was the number 3. Next to Missionary was 1.5. As I perused the list and saw how few of the boxes had been left blank, I began to regret my inability to remember any of it. There were positions on there that I hadn't tried in years, a few I'd never heard of (again I asked myself why I was so intent on moving on). 'You really let your hair down,' the woman offered sympathetically as she watched my eyebrows climbing closer to my hairline. 'You must have been through a great deal of stress.' I grunted, and then grimaced as the anvil in my head took a heavy turn.

At the bottom of the list, just above the eye-wateringly steep total fee, were a few rows beneath the word 'Other'. These, unlike the rows above, contained numbers on the left-hand side, written in the woman's childish handwriting, with the number 1 in each box in the middle and a particularly stratospheric fee in the right-hand column. It took me a while to work out what each of these was. The number 33 I could more or less guess, but what did 72 signify? And 689? Had there been another woman, and in that case why 689 and not 619? I avoided her stare, and as I handed over what was left of my cash, it occurred to me that if I was to continue my search I would have to sell the diamond. The woman slipped the money into her handbag and quietly left the room. I turned over onto my front and went back to sleep.

13

I awoke to find the anvil still irritably adjusting its position in my cranium. After removing the diamond from its tenebrous hiding place (the ability to dislodge precious stones easily from one's backside is one of the unexpected benefits of soft corpulence), I headed downstairs.

In the hotel reception I bumped into the driver. His matted yellow hair looked greasier than ever. 'I hear you enjoyed yourself,' he smirked.

'I did,' I replied. 'You were very kind.'

'You didn't really think the Hisbah would encourage the use of a prostitute, did you?' He glanced conspiratorially at the pretty receptionist, who was trying to suppress a grin. 'We help people to behave virtuously, according to the teachings of the holy Quran. We are not here to promote vice.'

I rolled my eyes and made for the exit, leaving him and the receptionist tittering in my wake. The doorman winked at me as I stumbled out. I ignored him, too busy dealing with the shock of the magnesium-bright sunlight that assaulted my face as I stepped onto the pavement. With no cash to pay for a taxi to the commercial district, I had no option but to walk.

Umfiki was not strictly a diamond town – the nearest mines were over a thousand miles away – but as a place that had come into money it attracted hustlers from all sorts of dubious industries.

Among those making the most of its coastal location were drug barons, people traffickers, ivory smugglers and arms dealers. There were counterfeiters, money launderers, internet scammers and illegal bookmakers. A whole market was given over to stolen mobile phones, another to stolen laptops. As an even shadier industry than most of these, I knew it wouldn't be difficult to find a dealer in precious stones.

The streets had a Wild West feel. Broad and dusty, they were flanked by long, wood-slatted, two-storey buildings whose balconies ran the length of the upper floor. Horse-drawn carts mingled with the clogged ranks of jeeps, Hummers and motorbike-taxis. Hawkers wove among the traffic pushing wheelbarrows or heavily-laden bicycles. There was bustle and noise at all hours of the day and night.

Most of the buildings were multi-purpose stores owned by Indians. The Indians had been here for generations, sometimes centuries, controlling trade routes into and out of the continent and colluding to undercut would-be competitors. Into and out of their gloomy grottoes passed an enormous variety of licit and illicit goods and people. The shelves were crammed with sundries, the floors a jumble of electrical goods, tools and cleaning materials. Cash was kept in a drawer beneath the counter (the Indians hadn't got to where they were by trusting banks), while the more valuable merchandise was hidden in back rooms or in the cobwebbed halls upstairs.

Exhausted by the walk in the simmering heat, I ducked into the first store I came upon. It was unlit and cool, like walking into a large cave. At its rear, behind a wooden desk fronted by a flimsy wire-mesh grille, sat a diminutive Indian. With his neatly trimmed, slightly forked white beard and Afghan-style fur hat he looked more like an Islamic cleric than a businessman, but this image lasted only until your gaze reached the garishness of his shirt. The shirt depicted red, Tahitian-looking women swinging on hammocks strung from yellow palm trees. The tops of the trees were swaying in the breeze against a bright blue sky.

'It's beautiful isn't it?' the man said solemnly in English, catching me staring. 'A friend from the United States of America sold it to me. He describes himself as an aid worker, but he also has a good eye for a business deal. In the end I got it for a fair price, but he is a hard man to beat down.'

I introduced myself, and he stood to shake my hand. Regaining his chair he indicated that I should take a seat on the stool beside him. From the open drawer above his lap he scooped out a handful of banknotes and began to count them, passing their corners like rosary beads between his thumb and forefinger. Behind and above us, shelves were piled high with school exercise books, boxes of sweets, packets of biscuits and tubs of skin whitener. They were from Turkey, Oman, China and India, and to compensate for their indecipherable lettering each bore a picture of the product contained within.

'You don't look like an aid worker yourself,' he said, sombrely regarding my paunch. 'So how might I be of assistance?' His English was clipped and formal in the way of all Indians whose families had been here since colonial times.

'Actually I am an aid worker,' I replied, keen to appear respectable. When I told him who I'd worked for he nodded in approval.

'An exemplary organisation,' he said. 'Perhaps you are on holiday now?' He folded the wad of banknotes and wrapped it in a rubber band.

'Something like that,' I said, shifting in my seat. 'I needed a break.'

'Yes, I can imagine that such work must be taxing. My American friend told me that his business activities were a way of taking his mind off all the suffering he encountered.'

I pursed my lips and nodded.

'Would you like a drink?' he said. 'Have a cold drink.' He shouted, and a teenage African came in through the doorway. The boy was barefoot. His boss instructed him to fetch us each a can of Turkish cola from the generator-powered refrigerator in the far corner of the store. Despite the chemical taste, the cool liquid was a relief to my overheated innards.

The Indian stared at me, the expectant look in his dark, beady eyes making it clear he wanted to get down to business. I pulled out the diamond and handed it to him. With no sign of emotion on his face he took a pair of tweezers from the pocket of his shirt and held the stone up to the beam of light from the street. After turning it a few times he placed it carefully on a sheet of white paper on his desk and flicked on the lamp that stood in one corner. From the same pocket he pulled out a magnifying glass. Hunching his narrow shoulders, he bent to conduct a further examination.

'It's nice,' he said, still expressionless. 'You must have been well remunerated for your work.'

'It's all I have to show for it,' I said. 'You're looking at my life savings.'

His brow crinkled so slightly it was almost imperceptible. 'You know the market for diamonds is not what it was,' he said as I realised I'd been naïve to betray my desperation. 'The government controls everything these days.' He was still peering at the stone, his thin, bony face illuminated dimly by the light reflecting off the paper. His voice was quiet and calm. 'It is especially difficult to sell uncertified diamonds. Do you have the certification?'

He knew I didn't, but his face remained serious as he asked. He looked up and told me how much he would pay. I had no idea of the going rate and was sure I was being ripped off again, but a quick calculation in my head told me that what he was offering would be enough to cover double the girl's most recent asking price and to tide me over for a couple more weeks. I was no longer certain that it was money that would win the girl's favour, but I knew I needed money to find her. I knew too that I wouldn't be able to out-haggle this shrewd little man, who had by now switched off the lamp and picked up another pile of banknotes for counting.

A horse and cart edged across the bright frame of the doorway, carrying a mixed cargo of charcoal sacks and jerrycans. The soot-covered driver, perched on one of the sacks, was whipping and shouting at the horse, which was rendered helpless to advance by the dense traffic. A Land Cruiser driven by a stern-looking young white woman crawled forward in the opposite direction, providing momentary relief to the poor animal as the carter paused in his whipping to gawp at her. On the pavement outside the Indian's store, the African boy was shouting into a loudhailer, extolling the benefits of a new toilet brush from China to a posse of eager women.

'I'll take it,' I said.

'A wise decision,' the Indian replied. After binding up the wad he'd been counting and depositing it in the drawer, he took out a sheaf of loose notes and counted out the payment.

I pocketed the money. When I looked up I saw that he was watching me, his brow furrowed. 'And what will you do when this money runs out?' he asked. 'Return to your work with the charity?' He swept the diamond into the drawer, and I felt an emptiness in my gut at the realisation that I had nothing else to fall back on.

'That might be difficult,' I said, 'but hopefully something'll turn up.' Even after being robbed by the Hisbah police I had expected my funds to see me through a few more months, and after the episode with the prostitute from Moisture I hadn't had time to work out an alternative strategy.

He stroked his white beard. 'Perhaps I might be able to - how should I put it? - come to your aid,' he said with a little smile. 'A friend of mine has been thinking for a while about an interesting business project, and since I owe him a small favour I promised to help him if I had the opportunity. To implement the project we need the assistance of a European like you.'

'Like me?' I said, trying hard to think of a job specification that might encompass my attributes.

'Yes, we are looking for someone who knows how things work in Africa, and is not too...' He paused, frowning as he searched for the word. 'Let us say, someone who understands that one cannot always do everything by the book. My American friend would have fitted the bill perfectly, but he has no need of the money. And I have found that other foreigners in your industry are frequently rather high-minded.' I smiled, but his face remained inscrutable. 'It is difficult to know which of them one can approach with such an idea.'

'What's the idea?' I asked, thinking that some extra cash would be useful if the girl remained elusive.

'Do you mind if I call my friend? As my business partner, it would be better if he were involved in the discussions.'

'No problem,' I said. He picked up one of the three phones that were lined up on his desk and dialled a number. After a brief conversation explaining that he might have found somebody 'suitable for our project,' he replaced the phone and turned back to me. 'He will be here in ten minutes,' he said.

We sat sipping our colas, watching the busy street. At length he broke the silence:

'Your appearance here is well timed,' he said. 'Tomorrow I am due to leave Umfiki for a few weeks.'

'Going anywhere nice?' I asked inanely.

'I will travel, inshallah, far to the west of here, to the great African rainforests,' he said, draining his can and placing it carefully in the wastebasket by his feet. 'On business.'

'Diamonds?' I asked. Although the mines around Itongo had been stripped of most of their treasures, farther west could still be found large deposits of inferior stones, and the region was so

131

anarchic that there was no need for those prospecting there to worry about costly certification procedures.

'No,' he said. 'Buying diamonds in that part of Africa is dangerous, and I am no daredevil. I am going as a seller, not a buyer. There are untapped markets there, people who need my foreign-made products.'

'You mean rebels?' The place was awash with rebel armies.

He shook his head. 'As I said, I am no daredevil. No, I plan to trade with some of the pygmy tribes there. I think you Westerners call them hunter-gatherers. They are among the oldest inhabitants of Africa, but they are not so set in their ways that my twenty-first century merchandise will not be of interest to them.'

Impressed by his lack of sentimentality, I couldn't suppress a chuckle. I asked him what he thought the pygmies were after.

'A variety of products,' he said, his eyes glinting with a salesman's enthusiasm. 'I will take them mobile phones and children's training shoes to help them in their work, baseball caps and sunglasses to protect their eyes from the sun, and portable radios and cigarettes to pass the time between hunts. I will take sugar and packets of chicken stock to flavour the food they catch, and tinned meat and fish to tide them over during lean times. Maybe I will even take soft drinks – I have yet to meet an African who can resist a can of cola. These products will make their lives both easier and more pleasant, and since they earn plenty of cash from the ivory trade and from tourists searching for what they think of as "the real Africa", I expect it to be a fruitful relationship for them and for me.'

He was interrupted by the honk of car horns. Through the doorway we saw three Hummers with blacked out windows, which had managed to part the traffic. They pulled up in a row in front of the store, like horses outside a saloon. The boy, open-mouthed, ceased his sales pitch. Passers-by stopped in their tracks to stare at the enormous vehicles. 'He is early,' the Indian smiled, closing his desk drawer quietly.

Out of each of the cars jumped a pair of burly men in dark suits and sunglasses. Two men took up positions on either side of the store's doorway, facing the street; the others stood beside the Hummers. After a short pause a studious-looking young man in spectacles climbed out of one of the cars, carrying a large hardback notebook. Two heavily made-up young women climbed down after him. They were wearing tight blouses and black mini-skirts that hugged their ample buttocks. The hair of their wigs was parted at the side and smoothed across their heads like 1980s backing singers. One of the women opened the passenger door of the middle car. From it descended a round-faced, potbellied man in a kaftan whose variety of patchwork colours made the Indian's shirt look sober. He approached the store, followed by the young man and the women. The crowd that had formed in the street gaped.

The Indian rose to his feet and stepped round his desk to clasp the man's hand. They exchanged greetings, asking after each other's health, families, homes and businesses. Once they had established that all these were as normal, the new arrival turned to me. 'This is my friend, the Minister of Justice,' the Indian told me. 'Minister, this is Hodge, from Great Britain. As I told you, he is interested in helping us with our new venture.' As we shook hands the minister told me he was grateful that I'd waited for him.

'Take a seat,' the Indian said.

'Oh I can't stay long,' the minister replied, his voice loud and declamatory. 'I have a very busy schedule, as you know. Once I have conducted my business here I must visit the gas plant to discuss how to deal with the villagers evicted by Mr Hodge's compatriots. Then, this evening, I will fly to the great Christian kingdom in the north east, where my counterpart, who like me is a man with a strong interest in the law, has very kindly - and at no small expense on my part, I should add - arranged for me to see the Ark of the Covenant.'

'What's that?' the Indian asked.

'I suppose you heathens are ignorant of these things,' the politician said, smiling. 'The Ark of the Covenant contains the laws of God, carried down by Moses on tablets from Mount Sinai. For three thousand years, since it was brought to Africa by the son of King Solomon, nobody but its guardian monk has been allowed to see it. The country's current Minister of Justice, however, is a great innovator, and in order to swell his coffers – I mean his ministry's coffers - he allows those of his fellow African lawmakers who are willing to pay for the privilege to lay their eyes on its wonders.'

'I see,' the Indian said quietly. 'You will charge the trip to expenses, of course?'

'Of course! As you know, I need to keep hold of my own meagre salary so that I can help my friends when they are in need.' He winked at the Indian, who gave a small cough. 'More importantly, it is of great benefit to our country for its senior lawmaker to study the divine laws.'

'Indeed,' the Indian agreed. 'Although it seems to me that your friend is taking a great risk. Let us hope that a less scrupulous minister than you does not decide the tablets would be safer in his own country.'

'A Minister of Justice stealing?' The minister's little round eyes widened in shock. His acolytes, too, looked horrified. 'That would be a betrayal of everything our esteemed office stands for. No, no, I don't think we need to worry about that. But why should it concern you anyway?' He smiled at the girls. 'You heathens would surely be glad to see the foundations of our religion go up in smoke.'

The Indian remained calm. 'Perhaps you didn't know that Moses is a prophet in Islam, too?' he said. 'His teachings are revered by Muslims as well as by Christians.'

'I know, I know. I was only ribbing you. You are always so solemn, my friend.' The man laughed affectionately. He remained standing, his three minions huddled behind him. The Indian and I sat down.

'Perhaps you would like to explain our plan to our new friend,' the Indian said, clasping his hands in his lap.

The young man in spectacles opened his notebook and, his pen poised above the page, waited for his master to speak. East Africa, the minister began, resting his folded arms on his potbelly, had become a stopping point on the narcotics routes to Europe and North America, and his government wanted a slice of the pie. 'This is an important industry,' he said, 'and it is natural that our country should benefit from it. As you can imagine, drug traffickers are unreliable payers of taxes, but I have alighted on a different means of ensuring we obtain our rightful share.'

His plan was for him and his fellow ministers, whenever they flew on official visits to Britain, to take with them consignments of cocaine. 'We considered heroin,' he said, glancing at the Indian. 'Heroin is a high-value product, and large quantities of it are coming into the country from Asia. But for now the military is in control of that trade, and our president correctly pointed out that we would face a coup if we tried to appropriate it. Besides, we are not greedy – we just want to earn a little extra money to help us fulfil our duties to our nation. So after lengthy discussions we chose South American cocaine, which as I expect you have heard is brought through here these days from southern Africa.' The young women nodded while the young man frantically transcribed his boss's utterances.

The ministers, he went on, would transport the product in diplomatic bags, which were immune from customs searches. 'Even if anything were discovered,' he said with a smile, 'our colleagues in the British government would turn a blind eye. They know that if they are to continue extracting our natural gas they need our good will. But it is better to do these things discreetly. You know what these so-called activists are like if they get wind of something they regard as corruption. It is an excellent and innovative plan, I am sure you agree.'

I had once heard of a similar scheme involving a West African president who was later murdered for his troubles, but the minister looked so pleased with his idea that I decided it would be better not to question its originality. Instead I asked what they wanted from me.

'We want you to help us to distribute the product. Whenever one of us is to make an official visit, you will return to your country to receive the contents of the diplomatic bags from our aides when we arrive. Naturally, we will pay all your expenses as well as a salary. With your background in the aid industry, you must have contacts who would like to assist our continent's development by purchasing one of its major export goods. We know how much you aid workers like to indulge in a little nose-powdering to relieve the stress of your work.' He chortled, and his minions chortled with him.

Although less altruistic in intention than Hubert's diamond smuggling proposal, the minister's plan seemed both more straightforward and less risky. Going along with it would resolve my financial difficulties without demanding great effort, while the economic cushion it would provide would allow me to indulge in Moisture's many pleasures as often as I wanted. The search for the girl seemed increasingly unpromising. She hadn't been sighted for weeks, and I had no idea where she might be. In my frustration I had begun to doubt her. Could she really be so much more attractive than the girls with whom I'd spent the last two nights? Or than Mama Alison's fleshy thighs? Or than all the other girls at Moisture I had yet to encounter? If I put aside my search to work on the minister's project there was always the possibility of trying again later. By then I might have amassed sufficient funds not just to spread the net more widely, but to be sure of being able to afford her once I finally found her. It even crossed my mind that if I suspended my pursuit I might recover from my strange and probably pointless fixation, and regain the serenity of old.

'So, what do you think?' the Indian, stroking his beard, broke the silence.

'It's a good idea,' I said. 'I think it can work.'

The Indian nodded. The minister stared at me.

'But I'm afraid I can't help you with it,' I heard myself say, helpless to control the words that were emerging from my mouth. 'I can't leave Africa at the moment.'

The Indian and the minister looked at each other, their eyebrows perched high up their foreheads. 'But you told me you were on a break,' the Indian said.

'From aid work, yes, but I have other things I need to do.'

'Other things?' the minister said.

Assuming they had probably seen her, and would therefore sympathise with my plight, I told them about the girl.

The look of surprise vanished from the minister's face. He sighed deeply. Even the Indian looked wistful. 'I understand,' said the minister. 'The girl you speak of was indeed a great beauty. Her eyes … they shimmered like a mirage, like the haze that used to hover over the hot springs at the southern tip of Africa before they were paved over for a mall. But it was not just her appearance that was so extraordinary – she was beautiful without being proud, dignified yet humble, kind to those in need. It was no wonder so many people gave up their business to go and see her - even old stick-in-the-muds like our friend here,' he gestured towards the Indian. 'She was not an ordinary mortal.'

The Indian agreed. 'Her eyebrows,' reflected this taciturn man who a few minutes earlier had been talking about selling canned fish to pygmies, 'their crescents were as exquisitely defined as the wings of a swift.'

'We never see swifts anymore, do we?' the minister mused.

'We do not,' the Indian replied. 'They no longer need to come to Africa for winter. It is hot enough for them in Europe.'

'Where did you see her?' I asked. Although no less an authority on the subject than Mama Alison had told me the girl was not in Umfiki, I was still finding it difficult to believe she had never set foot in what seemed a perfect place to ply her trade.

'In Tishioni, like everybody else,' the minister said, looking suddenly mournful.

'She refused him,' the Indian told me. 'He offered five times the price we had heard she was asking, but as soon as she saw the money in his hand she said she was feeling ill and left. We never saw her again.'

I looked at the minister for confirmation. 'It's true,' he said, grasping his elbows with his pudgy hands. 'I would have paid ten, twenty, one hundred times the asking price, but she is more elusive than the Ark of the Covenant – until my counterpart took office, that is. She never came back. Maybe like the Ark of old she is only to be enjoyed by one man.' His dreamy gaze tilted upwards, settling on the shelves of sundries high above my head. His little eyes glimmered as his voice dropped to a whisper. 'And what a fortunate man that will be.'

Something in my stomach seemed to do a backflip. To the minister's prophecy I paid little heed, but the girl's refusal to accept his money was more serious. If even an African government minister couldn't afford her, I knew I was in trouble.

The Indian was shaking his head. 'I think you were the fortunate one,' he said to his friend. 'If she was a woman like my wife she would have caused you only torment. I have been married for two months, and she has never once stopped haranguing me.' He sighed, and the minister, who had recovered from his brief bout of melancholy, laughed in the weary manner of one who had heard the diatribe many times before.

'And if they are not cruel they are treacherous,' the Indian continued plaintively. He turned to me. 'This woman is my second wife. And my last. The first went off with my former assistant, a barefooted African boy like that one. She met him at our wedding. If I were you I would call off my search right now. Women are nothing but trouble. I thank Allah the most merciful that tomorrow I will escape her for a while.'

'Enough of your complaining,' said the minister. 'Let us get back to business. I am a very busy man. And you,' he turned to me, 'forget your pipe dreams. You will help us with our project, will you not?'

I spread my arms and shrugged. 'I'd love to,' I said. 'It sounds like an excellent plan, but I've come too far. I can't give up now. Can't you use your consul?'

'We cannot. Unfortunately our consul is under a cloud at the moment. The British suspect him of involvement in smuggling Africans into their country. As you know, while your great nation rolls out a red carpet even for criminals from overseas as long as they are wealthy, migrants who are honest but poor are beyond the pale.'

'Well as I say, I'd love to help you, but –'

'You have, have you not,' the minister interrupted, 'just sold an uncertified diamond to my friend here?' He was still smiling, but his eyes had lost a little of their friendliness. 'And you have not forgotten, I am sure, that I am the Minister of Justice, and that trafficking in illegal diamonds is a serious crime, punishable by many years in jail.'

The young man stopped writing in his notebook and looked up at me. The Indian stared down at his clasped hands. I was trapped again. I suddenly felt exhausted, and it occurred to me that it would be easier just to cave in to his wishes. I took a deep breath.

'I know somebody in England who can help you,' I said. I had thought of my friend Jules when Hubert had suggested the

139

diamond smuggling business, but drugs were a much better fit for his talents. I had met this bon vivant several years previously when he was working as an international development consultant. He specialised in conducting audits of aid projects, and Feed Africa Today often hired him to rubber stamp its activities. Aid agencies would usually carry out these audits themselves, giving themselves glowing reviews for their work, but when they wanted to confer on them a veneer of objectivity, they hired people like Jules. These consultants knew on which side their bread was buttered ('we are parasites on the parasites,' Jules would admit over a glass of his favourite imported claret), so they too awarded the projects high marks. Although the recommendations section of their reports would usually contain a few suggestions for improvement, rare was the consultant who didn't guarantee himself repeat business by calling for a project's funding to be renewed.

This tribe of wandering pundits made a good living even by aid worker standards, and Jules was no exception. He was famed in the industry for the lavish dinner parties he would throw in whichever five-star hotel his client had selected for his stay. He would requisition a private banquet room and a section of the kitchen, where his cook would prepare six-course meals bursting with fish, fowl and the exotic African game of which Jules was so fond. The imported wine, which he instructed the waiters should gush like the Congo into the Atlantic and which was complemented by sand dunes of cocaine, had eventually taken its toll on Jules's health, and he had returned to Kent to work as an adviser to the British government. With his high-level connections and the network of gluttonous friends who attended his dinner parties back home (a network which included more than a few burnt-out former aid workers), he was ideally placed to assist the minister with his scheme.

When I listed Jules's credentials the minister was impressed. He told me to call him there and then, so I took out my phone (so old and cheap that the Hisbah police had not bothered to relieve me of it) and dialled his number. Jules was pleased to hear from me. He had been waiting for me to get back in touch, he said. When I told him about the girl, he asked if her juices flowed like the Zambezi as it tumbled from the Victoria Falls' rim (in the days, he must have meant, before drought slowed the river to a trickle). He was delighted by the minister's suggestion. Living in England, he said, without *per diem* payments and where everything except his daily rate was many times dearer than in Africa, had forced him to rein in his expenditure, and his parties were in danger of losing their legendary reputation. 'When do I start?' he said, 'and what's my cut?' Not without a little envy that my friend was to benefit from a windfall that could have been mine, I handed the phone to the minister, and went out to wait in the street while they negotiated.

14

I wasn't sure what to do next, so I stayed in Umfiki. I had no leads as to the girl's whereabouts, and there was no obvious alternative destination she might have chosen. As a booming, busy city to which thousands migrated every week from less prosperous parts of Africa, Umfiki seemed as likely as anywhere else to yield the information I sought.

After a long debate with myself about whether to return to Moisture, I resolved to avoid the evenings, when there were more girls on offer and a higher risk of squandering the little money I had left, and to visit only in the afternoons.

Mama Alison received me with the warmth she afforded her most lucrative clients. 'I heard you had a good time with one of my girls,' she said as she showed me to a cushioned seat in the bar, her toothy smile tinged with only the faintest of smirks. 'She is one of my most valued employees.'

'I can't remember much about it,' I said.

She laughed. 'You did seem a little the worse for wear. You must be a wealthy man to be able to afford so many of her services. Warthog and gin, was it?' She beckoned the barman over.

'Just a Warthog,' I said. 'I'm not so wealthy now.'

The sparkle in her eyes dulled. 'Well, I will leave you to relax,' she said. 'I have business to attend to. If you need anything, ask my barman to call me.'

After a few days indulging in a comfortable but chaste routine, my beer-fuelled afternoons sandwiched by inexpensive but hearty African meals, I began to grow restless. I had heard nothing about the girl except the eulogies of those who had trekked to Tishioni to see her, and I knew that the longer I dallied, the greater was the danger that I would lose her trail for good. Already worried that she might have slipped irrecoverably from my grasp, I decided that if I was to have any prospect of finding her I would have to extricate myself from Umfiki's grip.

I had only a single straw to clutch at. After concluding his discussions with Jules, the Minister of Justice had suggested I visit a farm he had acquired a hundred miles or so from Umfiki. Although the farm was a long way from any large towns, he said, it was close to the junction at which the road leading southwest from Tishioni met the westward road from Umfiki (the only other route out of Tishioni that I hadn't travelled on led north into Kaaba United territory). If the girl had bypassed Umfiki, the minister assured me, she could not have avoided the junction.

I had thanked the minister for the offer but told him I didn't think it would be necessary. His idea had sounded devoid of promise; a few more days in Umfiki, I thought, could hardly fail to throw up something more concrete. Now, however, I had nothing else to go on, so I called the number he had given me and told the grouchy-sounding man on the other end of the line that I would be paying him a visit.

The farm turned out to be both farther away – the journey took a whole day, in four different bush taxis – and more remote than I had been led to believe. It wasn't just that there were no towns nearby; it appeared that there wasn't even a hamlet within several dozen miles. The land, moreover, seemed poor – parched fields dotted with dry baobab trees, peasants tilling the hard soil with hoes in the still-fierce early evening heat. Only the low trill of crickets broke the encompassing arable silence. As I trudged up the long track to the farmer's cottage, I reflected despondently that if the girl had come this way, she would undoubtedly have passed through quickly.

The cottage sat on a small rise. It was constructed of unpainted planks of wood under a corrugated-iron roof. The planks were neatly planed and cut, suggesting the work of a skilled carpenter. Overhanging the roof were the leafy branches of an acacia, the only tree for miles around. A ribby grey horse snoozed in its shade.

'I built it with my own hands.' A thin, long-legged man with a dark face and a smudge of white hair was watching my approach. 'He wouldn't give me anything towards it - I had to find all the materials myself. That man is tighter than the grip of a rock python.'

'Where did you get the wood?' I asked, looking around at the desiccated landscape. I dropped my bag beside my feet and pushed my hair, lank and damp after the walk from the junction, back from my forehead.

He pointed to the south, where far off in the haze a line of low hills rose like a rumple in a rug from the scorched plain. 'There was a patch of forest left over there,' he said. 'I sent my peasants for it.'

Despite the heat, the man's blue baseball jacket, which bore the logo of an American college team, was zipped up to his lightly bearded chin. He stood in the doorway, looking unwelcoming. I introduced myself.

'I guessed,' he said. 'You'd better come in.'

He led me into the single room that constituted his house. It was dark and cool, with a thin foam mattress on a low bed in one corner and a carved wooden armchair with cushions in another. He instructed me to sit on the chair, and stood before me while we talked.

His name was Ossie. The minister had hired him a couple of years previously to look after his farm. The lawmaker had bought up thousands of hectares in the hope of selling them on to investors from China or Korea whose own countries' soil was no longer cultivable. The land was almost barren, but to give the appearance of fertility when the Asians came to visit, Ossie had been charged with overseeing a small band of peasants who would turn over the earth and cover a few of the fields with hardy cassava crops. 'He thinks the Asians are fools,' the old man said, his tone still grumpy. 'He's probably right - they've been buying up land like this all over Africa.'

He had seen the girl, he said, but many months ago. Still he remembered her. 'I am old and frail,' he explained, 'and my body lags behind my mind, but desire will be with us until the end.' Standing tall, his face made golden by the soft radiance from the window above my head, he looked out over the flat fields. 'It is no wonder so many men came to blows over her,' he said quietly. 'She was the most beautiful woman I have seen in all my long life. Her bearing was so calm, so serene, as quiet as a fish eagle's glide. Before the fish eagles disappeared, I mean – before they ran out of fish to eat. And her eyes, her eyes -'

'Did she pass this way?' I interrupted, unable to wait to hear him out.

'As I told you, it was many moons ago. I was on my way home from a meeting with the minister and the Asians in Umfiki. A terrible place. That was the first time I'd ever left this plain, and it will be the last too. The road is two miles away from here, but my peasants would have informed me if she'd passed by since.'

My last resort was beginning to look like the end of the road. The girl appeared to have travelled along none of the thoroughfares leading from Tishioni, and for the first time since I'd first heard about her back on the island, nobody had any notion of where she might have gone. Had her rumoured illness taken a turn for the worse? Had she been kidnapped by Kaaba United and kept or sold as a sex slave? I began to wonder if she even existed, or if it was all, as the Minister of Justice might have been hinting, a mirage, a wild goose chase, the product of a fevered mind rendered delirious by spending too long in the tropics.

I slumped farther down into the armchair, my fingertips grazing the floor. My face, I noticed, was so hot that most of the sweat pouring down it evaporated before it reached my chin.

'You don't look well,' Ossie said. 'I'll bring you water.' He dipped a tin cup into a bucket by the door. I gulped it down and asked for another. The light from the window was weakening, the room growing cooler, but still I was sweating like a galley slave. Ossie brought me a lump of pounded cassava in a bowl. I picked at it feebly, but for once had no appetite. I felt drained of strength, and before long fell asleep.

I didn't wake until late the next morning. The sun was glaring in through the window above my head. A blanket that the old man must have draped over me was lying in a heap on the floor beside the chair. My brow and scalp were awash with sweat, and the sinking feeling that came over me as I realised where I was did nothing to help revive me.

Ossie came in from the fields and asked how I was feeling. 'You need to see my friend the witch doctor,' he said matter-of-factly. 'His medicines will restore your energies, and he'll be able to tell you where this girl of yours has gone, too.'

I laughed weakly. 'I'm not a great believer in witch doctors,' I said. Although I wasn't one of those who dismisses these medicine men's powers out of hand – if their curative abilities were useless, I doubted their profession would have endured for so long - I had little time for their claims to clairvoyance.

'He's a very powerful man,' Ossie said, undeterred. 'He will be along one of these nights to bring me medicine for my old bones. I have no doubt he'll be able to help you.'

I told him I didn't have much money left.

'Oh, don't worry. You won't have to pay. You're a friend of the minister's, and the minister is one of his best customers. The doctor helped him to get where he is today, and has been well rewarded for it. He recently got back from a long journey which took him halfway across Africa to find new medicines, all funded by the minister. He'll help you as a favour to his client.'

I felt too lethargic to protest. When the witch doctor appeared a couple of nights later, I was still too weak to get up from the armchair. Tall and thin like Ossie, the man stooped as he came in through the door. He wore a striped red and blue robe with a hood which hid his face. He carried a leather satchel over one shoulder, and a thick wooden stick hung from his belt.

The two men took seats on the bed. The witch doctor, who had not lowered his hood on entering the room, pulled a glass jar from his satchel and tapped powder from it onto a twist of paper. Ossie slipped the paper into the pocket of his jacket and began to tell the man about my plight. The silky material of his robe glowed in the light of the single candle that was the house's only source of illumination. I couldn't see his face as he looked over at me, but while he listened he was nodding as if none of this was news to him.

'I have seen such cases before,' he said when Ossie had finished. 'On my way back from my trip I stopped in Itongo and had to treat a young lad there who was suffering the same symptoms, and for the same reason.'

'And you cured him of course,' Ossie said, looking over at me.

'I cured his fever, but he wouldn't let me treat his obsession. He was happy in his infatuation.'

'Was he a diamond miner by any chance?' I asked.

'He was. He was mining with his father, a famous warlord. But how do you know him?'

I told him I'd been to Itongo too.

'I see you have travelled far for this girl,' he said. 'Perhaps I can help you to find her.'

'I doubt it,' I said. 'Nobody has any idea where she is.'

'Maybe nobody around here has such information, but my journey to the west was not in vain. I acquired not only new medicines, but new knowledge and equipment to which doctors in these parts do not have access.'

'Yes,' said Ossie, whose demeanour had lost all its former grumpiness. 'Tell him, tell him.'

'My destination,' the witch doctor continued gravely, 'was just a little to the west of the very centre of Africa. It is not a place that is widely known, merely a small village. But the village contains the ruins of a house that once belonged to one of Africa's greatest prophets.' Ossie rubbed his little white beard thoughtfully. I stared mutely at the candle, wondering whether I would ever recover the strength to resume what seemed an increasingly futile search.

'This prophet was a fisherman,' the witch doctor continued. 'He was a follower of Jesus, like yourself.'

I let out a little snort.

'Like Jesus, he performed many miracles. He sat on rocks and drove them around as if they were cars. He caught a catfish – in those days there were still fish in the central African lakes - which told him that before he died he would pick up the earth and take it to heaven, rolled up like a sleeping mat. His stick, a simple hoe handle like this one in my belt, could fell his enemies and turn their bullets into water. But his enemies did not die, for like Jesus he was a man of peace. The French were enslaving his people, and in their desperation to be free of their oppressors his people chose him as their leader. He knew that he could evict the colonisers using his magical powers - the bees of the forest, he told his followers, would be invincible when directed against the enemy – so he exhorted his followers not to use force.'

I hadn't heard of this particular prophet, but stories of bullets being turned into water and bees used as weapons of war were common in the mythology of anti-colonial struggles. Like those other tales, this one ended badly.

'His followers did not believe him,' he went on, shaking his hooded head sadly. 'In this way too he was like your Jesus. Their faith was not strong enough. They chose to use violence instead to drive out the French, and the French gunned them down.'

'What happened to the prophet?' Ossie asked.

'He was killed too, but some believe he has already come back to life once, and that he will one day come back again to fetch up the earth.'

'Already come back to life?' Ossie rubbed his beard harder.

'Yes. When he caught the catfish, it was late in the evening and very dark. After the fish had spoken to him, he saw in the sky a shooting star, which fell to earth not far from where he stood. Many years later another leader of men, who was also trying to drive out the French, fell to earth in exactly the same spot, the victim of a plane crash orchestrated by the colonisers. This man, his people believe, was the first reincarnation of the prophet.'

I shook my head in weary disbelief. Ossie shook his in awed admiration.

'So it is a place of great power,' the man said. 'And with the tools and knowledge I have brought back from it I will be able to help you.'

He rummaged in his satchel and pulled out a shard of mirror. 'Let me see, let me see,' he said. 'This glass should tell us exactly where to find her.' He held it before his face and peered into it. Ossie stared raptly over his shoulder. The room was warm and muggy in the darkness. A moth the size of the palm of my hand flapped around the glass bottle that held the candle. Slouched in my armchair, I numbly watched its shadow playing on the walls.

'Here she comes,' the witch doctor mumbled as Ossie leaned in closer. 'Yes, here she is. You see her?' Ossie peered closely at the mirror, but his face remained blank. I yawned.

'She is here, oh yes she is indeed beautiful. She is lying down, you see?' Ossie still couldn't see. 'Look at her, look at her hair. How

149

closely cropped she wears it – you can tell she is special, no wigs or hair extensions for her. And look at her cheekbones, they are as high as the leap of the dama gazelle, that exquisite antelope that once foraged in the western deserts before it was hunted to extinction.' I rolled my eyes. Ossie was looking at the witch doctor now, having given up on the mirror. But the man continued to talk.

'It seems she is in poor health.' I looked over, startled. 'She is very thin. But look at her eyes, how they sparkle. Come and see her.'

I shuffled over and collapsed onto the bed beside him. He showed me the mirror, without turning it towards me. I am not sure whether it was the flickering shadows or my muddled state of mind, but I thought I could make out the shape of a woman's head, grainier even than the photographs I'd seen on the island, but with two bright lights shining where the eyes must be. For a few seconds my heart pounded against my ribs like a caged bull, but when I squinted to try to bring her into focus the image disappeared, and the mirror went black.

The witch doctor, whose hood-enshrouded face was as hard to see as the girl's had been, was unperturbed. 'Now we must find out where she is,' he said, in the manner of a teacher describing the next step in a chemistry experiment. Ossie, who although he had not seen the image himself was triumphant that I had, nodded enthusiastically. 'Yes,' he said. 'I told him you had great powers. I think now he's starting to believe me.'

The man delved once more into his satchel, and fished out a handful of cowries. Seeing these little folded shells, the divining tool of charlatan clairvoyants all over Africa, I again rolled my eyes. The sighting of the girl, I realised, had been a feverish illusion. As he cast the shells onto the floor, I slumped back against the wall to the rear of the bed and left them to it.

'The pattern of the shells tells me she ran away from her village,' he said, stating the obvious. 'It seems that an important personage wanted to marry her, a politician perhaps.' Ossie looked at me, but although this story echoed what the British writer had heard, it still seemed nothing more than a lucky guess. 'She has travelled far and wide,' the witch doctor continued. 'She has ranged across the continent.' Ossie was nodding sagely. I was watching the moth as it divebombed the guttering candle.

'But where is she now?' the seer, who seemed to be enjoying himself, asked his audience. He peered down at the shells, and slowly bowed his head towards those that were closest to his feet. He lowered his voice: 'Ah yes, she is here, in a village not a week's walk from here.'

'A village?' Ossie said. 'What would a girl like her be doing in a village?'

'That I cannot say. I can only tell you where she lies. To get to this village you must travel south from here, and when you come to a long line of low hills –'

'The hills where I found the wood for the house,' Ossie interrupted, looking round at me.

'When you come to the line of hills you must climb to the top and descend on the far side. But do not go down as far as the cultivated fields at the bottom. You must descend only to the path that traverses the hillside above them. You must follow this path in an easterly direction, until it drops down to cross a dry river.'

The moth had settled on the neck of the bottle. Fatigue was spreading like a warm blanket over my body. Still the witch doctor droned on, with what I had to admit to myself was an impressively-detailed flight of fancy.

'You will finally come to another dry river, which you must follow until it splits into two. She lies not far from here, not far at all.'

'What's the name of the village?' asked the helpful Ossie.

The medicine man pondered. 'That too I cannot tell you. The shells withhold secrets even from the best of us. I can tell you that you must take the rightward branch of the dry river, and that soon after you will come to a forest. No, not a forest. Perhaps once it was a forest. Now it is a small copse, a copse containing an exceedingly rare tree, an ancient mulberry with thick foliage and pale green fruits hanging from its branches. This tree is the last of its kind, the only one still standing. Its roots, you see, are a powerful aphrodisiac, so in these gluttonous times the species had no chance of survival.' Ossie was looking over at me again as he took it all in. 'In that copse, or very near to it,' the witch doctor continued, 'lies the village where you will find your girl.'

My eyes closed slowly in sleep.

15

By the morning the doctor had gone, but he had left a small jar of lilac-coloured powder with Ossie for my fever, as well as a red paste for the sore on my thigh. At Ossie's insistence I took a spoonful of the powder mixed with water. By the following day I felt better (Ossie again looked triumphant), and taking my leave of my host I set off for the junction to await transport back to Umfiki.

It was another staggeringly hot day, and by the time I had completed the two-mile walk I was as usual lathered in sweat. The only signs of life at the junction were a couple of market women squatting in the dust and a tea shack made of old grain sacks daubed with aid agency logos. A hot, dry wind blew in gusts over the surrounding plain, stirring up the black plastic bags discarded by those who had passed through. There was not a vehicle in sight.

Knowing I might have to wait many hours for a lift, I pushed aside the curtain of the tea shack and lowered myself onto the rickety wooden bench inside. To my surprise the skinny old woman crouching by the kettle in one corner had another customer. Sitting at the far end of the wooden bench, he too was old and thin, with the bony face and veiny neck of an ascetic. His attire, by contrast, was luxuriant. He wore a long, flowing white robe, its lower folds splayed about him like a bridal gown on the dusty ground. On his head was a leopardskin cap, and at his waist hung a thick black flywhisk with a bone handle. The tiny skull of a monkey, its lower jaw missing, dangled from a leather cord around his neck. He was sipping frothy green tea from a small glass, his large, sunken eyes half-closed as coils of steam ascended his gaunt cheeks. I had never met his like before, but I knew his outlandish garb could only be that of a traditional priest.

'We are graced by the presence of a foreigner,' he said to the woman without looking at me, his voice gravelly and dry like the plain. 'Kindly give him a glass of hot, sweet tea and your tenderest coconut bun, and add them to my bill.'

The woman, squatting on her haunches, lifted the dented tin kettle from its charcoal-filled tray and poured me a glass. She made to wrap a fried bun in a scrap of paper, but I raised my hand to stop her – although I was feeling better I still had no appetite.

I thanked the man, and to make conversation in this lonely redoubt asked where he was headed.

'To Tishioni,' he said, 'if the gods will it.'

'I doubt Allah wills it,' I said flippantly.

'Oh, even in Tishioni there are those who follow the old ways,' he replied with a smile. 'Even among those who call themselves Muslims or Christians there are many who still respect the spirits, and many, too, who seek my intercession with the ancestors. My flock is diverse – I minister to pastors and imams, who will never take an important decision without asking the gods of Africa for guidance. And what about you? What brings you to these arid lands?'

Although I knew the likelihood that either he or the tea woman had seen her was minimal, in my desperation I told him about the girl.

'You are chasing a girl through the wilds of Africa,' he said, 'purely for the sake of copulation?'

I told him it was not just about sex, but a combination of things. I could no longer remember exactly why I had embarked upon the pursuit, but I knew I wouldn't be able to rest until I found her.

'Perhaps it is a spiritual quest?' he said. I slurped at my tea, wondering if this was about to become a sermon. The woman had placed the kettle back on its tray. Outside, a cricket began its daily whirr. 'It seems to me that you are a lost sheep, seeking redemption. This is noble. Like all of us, you no doubt have sins to atone for, and the ancestors look kindly on those who admit the error of their ways. But this girl, you say, is a prostitute. I do not like to judge my fellow men, but a prostitute is a strange choice as an object of pilgrimage.'

'She's not an ordinary prostitute,' I said, reluctantly allowing myself to become dragged into a discussion, 'but even if she was, I don't see that prostitutes are less worthy of devotion than other people.'

He gave his drained glass back to the woman. 'That is an interesting point of view,' he said, 'and one that had never previously occurred to me.' He fingered the monkey skull pensively. 'In Africa, you see, prostitutes are perceived as sinners. But this is one of the positive results of the mixing of cultures, that each of us is exposed to new ideas that challenge our prejudices. You might expect a person in my profession to see only the negative side of such mingling, but I believe that as long as your spiritual foundations are solid, there is nothing to fear from foreign influences. The problem, as you will have seen on your travels, comes when you lack those strong foundations, or when they have been destroyed, as so often in Africa, by force. As you know, foreign influence in our continent has not always been peaceable.'

Surprised to hear these views from a man whose religion had taken such a pounding at the hands of foreign imports, and although I knew that my agreeing with him increased the risk that he would prolong his homily, I couldn't help but nod in sympathy. When he asked the woman for a second glass of green tea, it seemed my fears would be realised. She, too, appeared to be bedding in for a long lecture, although in her case with more enthusiasm. She took up the kettle, and stretching her arm above her head poured the steaming liquid into the glass she had placed before her on the ground. Not a drop fell outside the vessel's narrow rim. She picked up the full glass and another, empty one, and poured the tea from one to the other to cool it. After she had repeated this process half a dozen times a thick froth had settled on the surface. She passed the full glass to the priest, and took up another to pour a cup for herself. I was unprepared for what the priest said next.

'This girl you speak of is an interesting case in this regard. Her spiritual foundations seem strong. She has spurned many opportunities for wealth and comfort.'

I spluttered on my tea, spilling it onto my white shorts. 'You know her?' I said, in an unusually high voice.

'She appears uninterested in money, let alone in the knick-knacks foreigners have brought to Africa,' he continued, as if he had not heard my question. 'She does not even possess a mobile phone.'

The tea woman's head jerked back in surprise.

He sipped at his hot tea, absorbed in his thoughts, oblivious to the froth of shock, relief, excitement and near-panic that was sloshing around my inner organs.

'And yet,' he went on, speaking slowly, his gaze fixed on the dusty, once-black curtain fluttering lightly in the breeze, 'and yet, as I told her, she is putting these strong foundations under pressure, putting them at risk.' The woman's rheumy eyes were looking at him with admiration, although her expression betrayed no sign that she understood his words. 'She is unwell,' he said. 'Perhaps you had heard this. She shivers often and her fingers tremble – those fingers that are as delicate as were the reefs around Zanzibar before the coral crumbled to sand. And she is wracked by fever. I told her the shivers are a message from the ancestors, a sign of their displeasure. She has been far from home, far from the family, far from the dwelling place of the ancestral spirits. This can bring only trouble, however noble her motives. She understood what I was saying, but I fear it might be too late.'

He sipped again, his elbows on his knees. Between the fingers of his free hand he rolled the monkey's skull like a prayer bead. The woman cupped her glass with both hands but did not drink. Outside, the cricket had paused in its chirruping, leaving only the whisper of the wind. The priest's slow movements and low, monotonous voice, I noticed, were quelling the torment that had convulsed me. I was enveloped now by a warm, sombre calm.

'It is very difficult to resist,' he said, still watching the rippling curtain. 'Those tears in her eyes, the tears of the river spirits, the tears that will never flow.' He breathed in deeply, the dry air quietly rattling his concave chest. He exhaled a long, low sigh. 'Such beautiful eyes. It is impossible to hold her gaze without trembling, without your throat drying out like a drop of water on a desert rock.' His own eyes had welled up. The tea woman was wiping a tear from her wizened cheek. I felt as if a heavy blanket had been laid softly over me, as if the consoling hand of an unseen woman was resting gently on my brow. 'Who knows,' the priest said in a hoarse voice, 'if she will hold out?' The curtain fluttered up in a gust of wind, revealing the bleak plain beyond.

For what seemed like hours we sat in silence, each in his own thoughts, listening to the wind. Somehow the priest's words had reassured me, his low, rumbling voice filling me with a strange feeling of confidence. I had a strong sensation now – no doubt in part an after-effect of my illness - that my quest to find the girl would soon be over. 'Where is she?' I finally asked, convinced that his answer would be definitive.

For the first time since the subject of the girl had come up, he turned to look at me. His eyes were dry. 'I can only tell you where I believe she was going,' he said. 'I do not know for certain if she decided to stay there, but I think that it is there that you will find her.'

I nodded, in no doubt that he was right.

'It is a small village,' he said, 'too small to appear on any maps. You will find it to the south of here, beyond the hills. I am told that most of its inhabitants have left for the cities, but the few who remain know it as Cantwara.'

I thanked him, and picked up my bag and hat to leave.

'When you pass over the top of the hills,' he added as I pushed aside the curtain, 'do not descend all the way to the bottom, but only as far as the path that traverses the hills from west to east. You must follow this path in an eastward direction. Then ask someone on the way – they will point you to the right road.'

I frowned in surprise at the resemblance to the witch doctor's instructions, but, shrugging it off as a coincidence, I started walking south.

It was by now early afternoon, and the sun's heat was blistering. In this shadeless landscape I was glad of my old straw hat and my long-sleeved white shirt, but with the hills apparently many miles distant (although by no means the week's walk that the witch doctor had described), and with only the single bottle of water that like all expats I never travelled without, I knew I wouldn't get very far without wheels. This was disconcerting - my body had been through enough in the past few weeks without having heatstroke to deal with too - but I had no alternative. There was no transport going in any direction, and nothing for it but to keep going.

Providence was on my side. I had been walking for less than an hour (but was already sweating exuberantly), when an old man on a donkey-drawn cart overtook me on the road. He stopped and offered me a lift. He was going as far as the hills, he indicated. I took a seat beside him on the cart.

He made a clicking sound and his donkey resumed its slow trundle. His cart carried no produce. Using sign language and a local tongue of which I knew only a few words, he explained that because of the long drought the area had suffered there were no longer any goods to transport. 'The only thing I carry now is people,' he said, his old eyes resigned to his fate. 'Most of those who used to live here have left for the cities, but from time to time somebody wants a ride somewhere. This cart is the local taxi.' He chuckled quietly.

I didn't tell him about the girl. I knew where I was headed now and didn't want to hear anything else. The stories I'd been told about her of late had done nothing but make me anxious, and I was agitated enough by the prospect of finally seeing her without having to digest any more unsettling news. The journey passed mostly in silence, and by dusk we had reached the foot of the long line of hills. The old man dropped me outside the mud cottage of a peasant he knew, who agreed to put me up for the night. After gratefully accepting the few shillings I proffered, he continued on his way.

The peasant welcomed me into his unfenced yard and introduced me to his wife and five young children. Ignoring my protests, he insisted on killing one of the family's two scrawny chickens in my honour. While his wife boiled the meat in a clay pot on the ring of stones that served as her stove, he bent over his patch of land in the fading light, tilling the few square feet of soil that were not yet occupied by spindly cassava plants. The children sat around me, talking excitedly among themselves, unable to believe their luck that a white man had landed in their midst.

After dinner – the cassava meal and chicken eaten with our hands from a shared bowl - we turned in early. The peasant and his wife slept on the hard dirt floor after forcing me to take their string bed (the children shared a single foam mattress). My fatigue didn't help me to sleep. I couldn't stop turning over in my head the thought that I would the next day at last see the girl. Why I was so certain of this I wasn't sure. It might have been the animist priest's comforting tone or, more likely, the cumulative effects on my mind of the relentless heat, the gruelling journeys, my prolonged fever and the many other self-inflicted or externally-visited stresses. I hadn't yet reached the extremes to which the French colonisers had been driven, but there had been enough deviations from my normal thought patterns to make me wonder whether something in my head had gone awry.

Sure, then, that I would soon find her, I spent a good part of the night trying to plan what I would do when the yearned-for moment arrived. Now that I'd sold the diamond I had nothing to give her, and I was fairly certain that neither the colour of my skin nor the money I had left would be enough to win her over. All I had to offer, I realised, was my persistence. As I lay in the darkness, telling myself that there was nothing I could do and that it wouldn't be I who would seal my fate, I couldn't help but think about what I would say when I saw her, how I would explain my presence, whether I'd be able to keep calm, how she might react to me. Whenever I began to drift into slumber, a wave of what must have been adrenalin flushed through my body and brought me up short. It was nearly dawn before I slept.

16

The peasant roused me before the sun had made much headway across the sky. After refusing my offer to pay for his hospitality, he stood waving with his wife and children as I made my way uphill.

It was relatively cool at this early hour, and I hoped I would make it to the top before the sun attained maximum strength. There was no track up between the rocks and scrub, but the climb was mercifully gentle, and when I reached the summit after only a couple of hours of trudging my shirt was damp rather than sodden. I looked down the far side. On the path that wound along the side of the hill I made out a large, lumbering figure coming slowly in my direction from the east. The man's gait and bearing were vaguely familiar, but I shrugged off the idea that I might have seen him before as yet another symptom of my condition, and continued on down.

The descent was slow – in parts I had to hold onto rocks to avoid a tumble – and by the time I reached the path the sun was high in the sky. Although hot, however, I felt surprisingly fresh, and calmer than I'd felt for weeks. It was as if I'd had a full and comfortable night's sleep, rather than a couple of hours of tossing and turning. Again I wondered if this might be related to the *soudanité*, some kind of trick it played in relaxing the mind and body before coming down with extra force just as its victim began to feel cured. Or perhaps it was the knowledge that today I would see the girl – a confidence that itself seemed not a little delirious. Far below me a few peasants toiled listlessly over the hard brown earth of the flat fields. Beyond them the land melted into a white haze. I took a slug of water, wiped my brow and turned to the left.

'Hodge? Hodge, is that you?' The lumbering figure had appeared from around a swelling on the hillside. 'Well, well. It is you.'

I stopped in my tracks and peered at him, shielding my eyes from the sun. He too had stopped, his dark eyes fixed on mine. His heavy frame was cloaked in a pale blue kaftan (an impractical choice for a hill climb). His stare was as piercing as ever.

'Harry!' I croaked, astonished. It was the barman from the island. He stepped closer and hugged me, patting me on the back as if we had both suffered a bereavement.

'What are you doing here?' I asked, deep down knowing the answer. His embrace had sapped me of a little of my morning vigour.

'I've been to see *her* of course. Same as you.' His jowls trembled slightly as he spoke.

'But how did you find her? I've been looking for her for months.'

'Oh you must remember how much I love a good story,' he said, his gaze drifting towards the haze-melted southern horizon as his eyes filled with tears. 'I've heard so many of them I knew how this one would turn out, and once I'd got to the mainland and talked to a few people it didn't take me long to work out where she'd be. They're still talking about her on the island, you see, and after you'd put the idea in my head it got to the point where I couldn't bear to be the only one who hadn't seen her.'

'And you saw her?'

'I saw her, yes.' Although he had accomplished his mission, his voice held none of its usual cheer.

'And?' Sweating more freely now, I was trying hard to remain calm.

'And they were right. She is the most beautiful woman there has ever been. Even now.'

'What do you mean, "even now"?'

'Even now that her beauty has begun to fade. Even now that the only one who bothers with her is that farmer.'

He shook his head in what looked like disgust. The girl, he explained, had been living for several weeks in a house in a nearby village. The owner of the house, a young cowpea farmer, was taking care of her. 'She's not well,' Harry sighed. 'An infection I think, probably because she was so weak. You heard people stopped helping her out I suppose.' I nodded. 'Bastards – so much for African kindness to strangers. And the farmer says she's been getting worse. He's all she has left.'

'Who is he, this farmer?' I asked. 'Some rich landowner?'

Harry laughed. 'Rich? No, he's not rich. Nobody round here's rich except you. But he's a good man and a hard worker. And he looks after her.'

'Looks after her?' I frowned.

'Oh I don't know if he looks after her in that way,' Harry chuckled. 'You'll have to find that out for yourself.'

'Did you talk to her?' I said, my twinge of envy quickly swamped by awe at being in the presence of one who had seen her so recently.

'She was too tired to talk. Most of the time I was there she was asleep. She only woke up for a few minutes, but it was long enough for me to feel her eyes on mine, and that was enough for me - I didn't need to stay any longer. But you'd better get a move on. As I said, she isn't well.'

My energy was dissipating rapidly. I asked him for directions.

'If you keep on this path for an hour or so,' he said, 'you'll come to a dry river. Once you've crossed it, keep going for another couple of hours until you reach another dry river. Don't cross this one, but follow it as it bends eastwards until it splits into two. Then -'

'Don't worry,' I interrupted him. 'I think I know the rest. I take the branch to the right, don't I?'

Harry looked surprised. I now had no idea whether it was the *soudanité* or some other strange and mysterious force that was controlling my existence. 'Somebody else gave me directions a few days ago,' I explained, 'but I needed confirmation.'

We parted with a handshake and another hug, and he wished me luck. I told him I hoped I'd return to the island one day. 'I wouldn't bother if I were you,' he replied. 'There's nothing there now. I had to close the Dashiki. I couldn't afford to keep it open.'

He went on his way. I walked as fast as my overburdened legs would allow. I crossed the first dry river soon after midday, and reached the fork in the second in the middle of the afternoon. I had failed to keep to Harry's schedule, and was worried I would have to spend yet another night on the road. Since I hadn't seen so much as a mud hut for several hours, however, I had no option but to go on.

Fortunately, it was not long before I came upon what I assumed must be the village. It was nothing more than a scattering of mud houses, many of them crumbling back into the dust in a state of abandonment. The copse the witch doctor had described consisted of half a dozen lime trees dotted between the buildings (reassuringly for my crumbling sanity, there was no mulberry tree). The warm air was still and snug. The sun was on the wane, its light beginning to soften into late-afternoon mellowness. As I moved away from the dry river and walked among the houses, searching for signs of human habitation, great reverberating spasms radiated like depth charges from my lower chest to my limbs.

I had to lean against the wall of a house to compose myself. The convulsions were not something I was accustomed to, and I surmised, without wanting to waste my dwindling energy thinking too deeply about it, that they must be some kind of adrenalin tsunami left as a parting gift by my fever. I finished off the last drops of water in my bottle, and looked around.

There was nobody to be seen. The houses I had passed were empty, with no signs of recent occupation. The village appeared to have been abandoned, but still the paroxysms did not stop booming behind my ribcage. I closed my eyes, resting the back of my head against the mud wall, and breathed deeply. When I opened them a few minutes later an old woman was standing before me. Leaning on a stick, a faded black dress draped over her skeletal frame, she squinted at me through eyes thickened by cataracts. She looked concerned rather than surprised, and smiled faintly back when I greeted her.

'Cantwara?' I said.

'Can. Twara,' she replied in a deep croak.

'The girl?' I tried the lingua franca, although I knew she wouldn't speak it.

She looked at me for a few seconds, apparently studying my bloated, sweaty face. My question hadn't registered. I didn't know what to say next. High above us in the whitening sky, a pair of vultures circled on the early evening air currents.

I shrugged my shoulders, helpless. But at this she put her bony hand on my forearm and pulled me away from the wall. Surprised at her strength, I picked up my bag and hat and allowed myself to be led. She took me off to one side, along a dusty track between roofless ruins. Then, pulling my arm towards her, she turned me away from the sinking sun to face down another track. She pointed ahead between the buildings, to where the bowing branch of a lime tree arched across the path. Beyond this, at the end of the track, perhaps fifty yards from where we stood, lay a little, thatch-roofed mud house.

She mumbled something in her language, and waggled a finger, gesticulating towards the house. I smiled weakly, and she hobbled away. As I made my way up the path, mighty pangs lurched in my

165

chest like the swinging bells of a cathedral. I felt as if I was walking through thigh-deep mud - it was all I could do to place one leg in front of the other. Passing below the arch made by the branch of the lime tree, I saw that the dwelling the woman had indicated was in better condition than the others in the village. A simple rectangular block, the thatch of its roof was clean and tidy, its sturdy walls plastered with a new coating of mud that glowed in the late sun's honeyed light. Like its neighbours, it had a curtain for a door, a darker brown than the reddish walls around it. As I drew near, knowing that behind that thin cloth lay the object of the past few months of my life – and maybe of the months that remained of it too – I crumpled in a heap on the ground.

By the time I came to, dusk had begun to smudge the sky, and the heat had gone out of the day. A young man was crouching beside my head. His face was fresh and unlined, and he wore a simple red dashiki, with a yellow and blue pattern around the V-shaped collar. He was positioned to shield me from the weakening rays of the sun. In his hand he held a small calabash gourd, and as I raised myself onto one elbow he offered it to me and told me to drink.

The water was sweet and cool, and he watched with serene eyes as I drained the gourd. 'It must be the heat,' he said, apparently unsurprised by the presence of a prone, overweight white man on the hard ground that fronted his house.

'Among other things,' I replied. The clanging in my upper body had muted, and I was again blanketed in the calm I had felt that morning.

The young man sat quietly on his haunches, his forearms resting on his knees. The clear, still air was comfortably warm, and the sky had turned the pale peanut colour of the tropical African evening. High above - although lower than before and a little farther to the south - the two birds still soared. With the sun illuminating from below their white heads and tails I saw now, to my amazement, that they were not vultures but fish eagles. I had heard that these beautiful birds were extinct, and wondered whether this might be the last surviving pair, roaming far and wide in search of food. Soon they would find the sea, I thought, where there were still a few fish to keep them going. I felt pleased for them. When I turned back to the young man, I saw that he had been watching them too.

After some time he spoke. 'You've come to see her,' he said. It was a statement, not a question, in a tone that exuded understanding.

'How is she?' I asked.

He pursed his lips and emitted a sigh through his nostrils. 'Why don't you come in?' he said, sending a shiver down to my fingertips.

We stood up. To one side of the house a well-fed piebald horse shook its head with a snort. Against the front wall leant a hoe, its cracked blade smeared with red soil. The young farmer pushed aside the brown curtain and passed through the doorway. I took a deep breath and followed. The room was dark and cool, and I could at first make out nothing but a wide, pale-coloured chair standing against the opposite wall. The farmer guided me to it by the arm, and as my eyes adjusted to the gloom I became aware that beside me, within a foot of where I was sitting, was the dark shape of a bed.

I inhaled sharply, but although I could tell that there was a figure lying there, its head just below the arm of the chair on which my forearm rested, I could see no details. The figure's torso, apparently covered in a blanket, rose and fell almost imperceptibly, and I could hear the faint whisper of breathing. The farmer took a seat on the bed, beside the girl's waist. We sat silently with our thoughts in the darkness.

At length, after what seemed hours, she awoke. As her eyes slowly opened, the room was suffused in a warm glow. Suddenly I could see everything clearly, her unblemished, dark skin, her close-cropped hair, her lofty cheekbones and finely curved lips. Her eyes appeared lit from within, a burning intensity softened by the glistening film of tears that, I saw now, was there to protect her from the world's glare. My throat dried out, like water on a desert rock. My chest, which had lain subdued since my collapse outside, now felt about to burst.

The young farmer looked as overwhelmed as I was, and when she smiled at him, a smile of a purity I will never see again, I saw that clearly, too - saw that this was how it must be. I felt my own eyes fill with tears, a brew combining awe, relief, satisfaction and some other stronger yet still tremulous feeling, the whole tinged with only the faintest melancholy.

'We have a guest,' he told her gently.

When she turned her eyes to rest on mine I felt my parched throat constrict as if in a seizure. As she smiled again that untainted smile, I gasped for breath as my bulging chest pushed upwards. The farmer laid a calming hand on my newly-healed left thigh. Only after several seconds could I muster a weak, defeated smile back.

'Have you come far?' she said. Her quiet voice was as crystalline as the dawn air on the Mountains of the Moon.

I managed to tell her.

She smiled again, a smile that crumpled my heart. 'I am glad you made it,' she said.

'I'm glad too,' I whispered, tears tumbling down my cheeks.

She closed her eyes, and the farmer motioned that we should go outside. He held aside the curtain as I followed him out through the doorway.

Night had fallen, a half-moon providing the only light. We sat on a tree stump beside the house, staring into the darkness. I dried my face on the shoulder of my shirt. I didn't know what I was going to do next. It no longer mattered.

'Why here?' I asked eventually.

'This is her place,' he replied. 'She has nobody here now - they all moved away. But Cantwara is her village.'

I nodded slowly, having half-expected such an answer.

'What was it that she was holding?' I asked. Under the blanket I thought I had made out a square shape beneath her fingers.

'It's a book,' he said. 'A man who came here yesterday brought it for her. He said it would cheer her up.'

I smiled. The musky scent of woodsmoke wafted in through the night, accompanied by the low murmur of distant adult voices. 'And do you think she'll pull through?' I said. I turned to him, and as I looked at him sitting there in the darkness, leaning forward with his forearms on his knees, I felt certain that he was someone in whom I could place absolute trust.

He sighed, his young face gazing straight ahead. 'I hope so,' he said quietly, as a breath of air cooled our faces. 'If the spirits will it.'

Acknowledgements

The idea for African Beauty came about while I was living on Ukerewe Island in the Tanzanian half of Lake Victoria. The island was a magnet for sex workers, who came there to service fishermen. Normally, sex could be had for a dollar or two, but one day when I returned to the island from a trip to the capital, I heard rumours of a particularly beautiful woman who was charging ten times that. The woman had come to the island from eastern Tanzania, but her stay was brief because nobody could afford her fee.

I wrote about these rumours on Ukerewe Days, a blog I was keeping. A friend, John Pollock, suggested it would make a good article if I tracked the woman down to find out what was special about her and why she charged such a high fee. Thinking my wife Ebru might not be thrilled by the idea of me chasing a beautiful prostitute around Africa, I wrote this book instead.

Without John's suggestion and Ebru's support, the book would never have been written. Similarly, I have Lisa Foreman, David Steven, Godfrey Kilosa, Nathan and James Helsby, Nick Michelmore, Gemma Willis, Jane Frewer, Lewis Broadway and Charlotte, Max and Claudia Weston to thank for their encouragement and ideas, and Barry Campbell for the cover design. Francesca Washtell and Peter Gostelow also provided invaluable insights, while if my parents hadn't endorsed the project, it probably wouldn't have seen the light of day.

Printed in Great Britain
by Amazon

23465917R00101